PIE RATS

THE KING'S KEY

Cyclone Sea

THE CRESCENT SEA

Western Passage

DRUMSTICK ISLAND

PHOENIX ISLAND

Devil's Cliffs

SEA SHANTY ISLAND

RUINED CITADEL

King River

Silver Falls

Eastern River

West

ISLAND OF KINGS

Southern Passage

QUEEN ISLAND

CLAW'S REACH

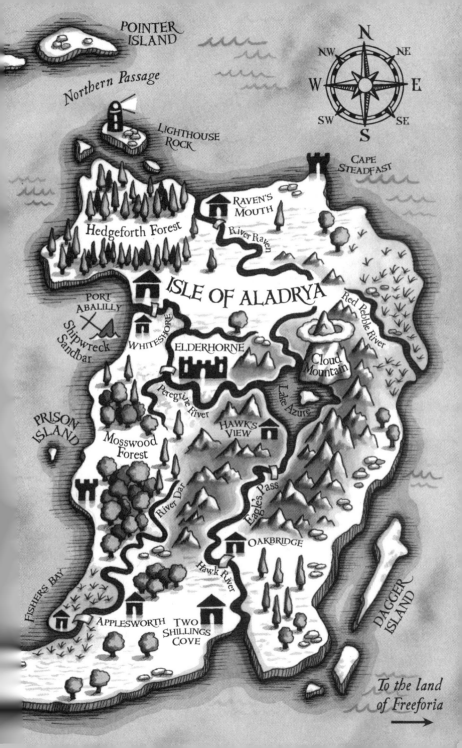

PIE  RATS

THE KING'S KEY

CAMERON STELZER

Illustrations by the Author

DAYDREAM
PRESS

For my brother, Tyson, inventor and encourager.
Here's to explosions of grand proportions!

First published by Daydream Press, Brisbane, Australia, 2014
Text and illustrations copyright © Dr Cameron Stelzer 2014
Illustrations are watercolour and pen on paper

National Library of Australia Cataloguing-in-Publication Entry
Author: Stelzer, Cameron, 1977 –
Title: The King's Key / by Cameron Stelzer
ISBN: 978 0 9874615 1 3 (pbk.)
Series: Stelzer, Cameron, 1977 – Pie Rats; bk. 2
Target audience: For primary school age.
Subjects: Rats – Juvenile fiction. Pirates – Juvenile fiction.
Dewey number: A823.4

Printed in China by Everbest Printing Co Ltd

Though the voyage may be long
and the waves may be fierce,
there is always hope –
Hope that land is but a blue horizon away
and one must keep sailing to find it.

Anso Winterbottom
Explorer, Discoverer and Adventurer

ONE

Guests

cratch, scuttle, rustle.

*S*The faint sounds woke Whisker from his dreams. He turned in his hammock, let out a sigh and drifted back to sleep.

SCRATCH, SCUTTLE, RUSTLE.

The sounds came again – much louder this time. Whisker opened his eyes and peered around the tiny cabin. Nothing stirred.

Perplexed, he swung his body from the hammock and lowered his feet to the floor. As quiet as a rat on a sleeping ship, he tiptoed past his two cabin mates and pressed his ear against the wall.

SCRATCH, SCUTTLE, RUSTLE. SCRATCH, SCUTTLE, SCRAPE.

The strange noises echoed through the wood, sending an itchy vibration down his body. He pulled his ear away and shuddered. *Something was out there.*

In growing fear, he turned to the sleeping figure of Hook Hand Horace and gave his friend a gentle shake. Horace opened one eyelid and gazed sleepily up at Whisker.

'Can you hear it?' Whisker asked softly.

SCRATCH, SCUTTLE, RUSTLE. SCRATCH, SCUTTLE, SCRAPE.

Horace's second eyelid sprang open and, with a sudden rush of adrenalin, his body lurched out of his hammock.

'Shiver me britches!' he gasped, landing hook-first on top of Fish Eye Fred.

'Ouch,' moaned the startled chef, brushing Horace aside with a mighty paw. 'Is it breakfast time already?'

'No, you oversized fish finger!' Horace exclaimed. 'We've got company!'

Fred dropped his huge feet to the ground and swivelled his enormous left eye in the direction of the sounds.

'Breakfast guests?' he enquired.

'*Uninvited* guests,' Horace replied, handing Fred a large fork. 'Let's show them some Pie Rat hospitality!'

Horace picked up a blue-handled scissor sword and headed for the door. Whisker hesitantly followed, thrusting a green scissor sword into his belt.

The three rats raced down the dark corridor. Horace hurriedly tapped each door they passed with his hook. Without waiting for a reply, the rodents leapt up the stairs and burst onto the deck of the *Apple Pie*. The entire deck was deserted.

Whisker scanned the ocean for clues. The silent wrecks of Shipwreck Sandbar surrounded the ship like a forest of statues, dark and foreboding. Strands of dry, brown seaweed dangled lifelessly from their rotting masts. A stiff breeze stirred up small waves, but neither wind nor water carried any sign of visitors.

It was only as the dim light of dawn began spreading through the sky that Whisker finally saw them.

His tail flinched behind his back.

Whisker's over-emotional tail had a nasty habit of acting on its own whenever he was anxious or afraid – and now Whisker was anxious *and* afraid.

'Steady on,' Horace whispered. 'Save your energy for the formal introductions. How many guests can we expect, Fred?'

Fred's powerful eye darted from left to right on a surveillance sweep of the ship.

'Ten to the left,' he grunted, 'and ten to the right.'

Horace looked relieved.

'I'm sure we can cater for twenty visitors,' he said, doing the maths.

'Um … there might be a few more,' Fred confessed. 'I'm only good with numbers up to ten …'

Whisker gulped as no fewer than *ten-times-ten* pale blue crustaceans emerged from the shadows. They came from everywhere, clambering over the wooden pastry-crust bulwark of the ship, scrambling out of barrels and dropping from the masts like webless spiders, ready to attack.

'Rotten pies to Blue Claw commandos!' Horace groaned, drawing his sword. 'I hope they're not expecting a buffet breakfast.'

The advancing soldier crabs got within striking range and suddenly halted. A crab wearing a blue beret raised his claw and spoke, 'By order of his exalted Excellency, the Honourable Cazban, Governor of Aladrya, you are hereby under arrest for heinous crimes committed against the State.'

Fred scratched his head with his fork, trying to fathom what the crab had just said.

'W-what crimes?' he mumbled.

'Piracy, theft, hooliganism ...' the crab rattled off impatiently. '... all-round anti-social behaviour.'

'ANTI-SOCIAL?' Horace cried in outrage. 'We're extremely social! Not that you empty-shelled mud eaters know anything about socialising.'

With the angry snap of claws, two hundred furious eyes glared at Horace. Whisker drew his sword and prepared for the inevitable.

'Don't worry,' Horace whispered. 'They're easier to fight when they're annoyed.'

Whisker wasn't convinced. His terrified tail twisted from side to side like an out-of-control cobra.

The crab with the armband raised his second claw. 'Attention, troops! I want the entire crew of this ship brought into custody – *dead or alive.*' He swept his claw through the air and, with the stampede of eight hundred frantic feet, the battle was on.

Horace was extremely short for a rat but his enthusiastic fighting style more than compensated for what he lacked in stature. Every move he made was doubled in intensity by his over-the-top running commentary.

'AVAST YE SCURVY SEA DWELLERS ... TAKE THAT, YOU OVERCOOKED CRAB CAKE ... FEEL THE HORROR OF THE HOOK ... ARGH, ME CRABBIES ... YOU CALL THAT A CLAW ...?'

Fred was a giant, and a strong one at that. He flexed his tattooed arm, shook his safety pin earring and hurled crabs overboard with his fork like they were nothing more than unwanted ants on a picnic table.

Whisker, the cyclone-surviving circus rat, had been rescued by the Pie Rats only seventeen days ago. He'd owned his scissor sword for exactly one hour and thirty-six minutes and for most of that time he'd slept. His sword-fighting skills were limited to one infamous move that involved cutting through a piece of rope. As the crabs pressed in around him, he knew he needed a plan – and fast.

What would Ruby do? he asked himself, annoyed that Horace hadn't knocked harder on the champion swords-rat's door. He thought back to the morning he'd seen her practicing on the deck. *There's got to be a move I can use.*

With a sharp nip to his tail from an attacking claw, the answer leapt into his head – *SPIN!*

Focusing all his energy on his stinging tail, he coiled it around the handle of his scissor sword and, imagining he was the world's first rat-tornado, began to spin on one foot. At first, his sword clanged awkwardly behind him, but as the spinning increased it rose into the air. One by one, the approaching crabs were sent flying into the ocean.

'Hurricane Whisker has arrived!' Horace cheered. 'Batten down the hatches.'

Despite Whisker's success, he knew there were two significant flaws in his tornado tactic. First, crabs can swim, and as soon as they splashed into the sea, they turned around and paddled straight back. And second, spinning leads to dizziness. It wasn't long before Whisker began to sway awkwardly from side to side like a spinning top losing momentum.

Just when he thought he was destined to join the crabs in an early morning salt bath, Whisker heard the buzz of tiny wings. He looked up to see a flash of green as Smudge, the loyal blowfly of the Pie Rats, launched an aerial attack with a piece of stale pie crust. The remainder of the crew bounded up the stairs behind him.

Mr Tribble

Emmie

Fish Eye Fred

Eaton

Hook Hand Horace

Whisker

THE PIE RATS
(and honorary members of the crew)

Captain
Black Rat

Smudge

Pencil
Leg Pete

Ruby Rat

Pencil Leg Pete, the runny-nosed Quartermaster, skidded to a halt on his red pencil leg.

'Oh my precious paws,' he gasped. 'Accidental decapitation by an apprentice is never advisable this early in the morning!'

Whisker grabbed a mast to stop himself spinning and promptly collapsed on the deck. He glanced up to see the swirling green eye of Ruby staring down at him, her crimson eye patch circling around her face. Whisker felt light-headed – and not just from the spinning.

'Nice move, *cyclone boy*,' Ruby smirked, 'I'll collect my royalty cheque later.'

'Oh, h-hi there, Ruby,' Whisker squeaked, sounding more like a deflating balloon than a roaring tornado. 'I-it's a l-lovely morning for a sword fight … isn't it?'

Ruby rolled her eye and turned to casually fend off an attack with two scarlet scissor swords. Whisker shut his mouth before more embarrassing words could squeeze their way out.

'Enough of this rat-foolery!' Captain Black Rat bellowed, striding into Whisker's view. 'Get those sails up quick smart before reinforcements arrive from the mainland. I want every paw on deck. And that includes the *honorary* members of the crew.' He glanced at the stairwell. 'Mr Tribble, are you down there?'

'Aye, Captain,' came a nervous voice from the stairs.

'You're on the wheel,' the Captain ordered. 'And the twins can assist with the sails.'

'Very well,' Mr Tribble sighed. 'Come along, Eaton. Come along, Emmaline.'

A middle-aged grey mouse with thick glasses emerged onto the deck with two small mice sporting matching school blazers.

'Ooh! A real pirate battle!' Emmie cried excitedly. 'This is the best school excursion ever!'

Her twin brother Eaton looked far less enthusiastic.

'This way!' the Captain ordered, booting an advancing crab overboard. 'Whisker will show you the ropes.'

Whisker brushed the unruly fur out of his eyes, straightened his one-sleeved shirt and staggered to his feet as the two mice rushed over to the giant cutlery masts.

It was a difficult job tying knots, doubling as a body guard and fighting soldier crabs at the same time; but with an energised tail and two able assistants, Whisker managed to raise the T-shirt mainsail, the handkerchief foresail and the underpants jib-sail without death, amputation or crab-claw lacerations.

Nearby, Ruby fought to keep the middle of the deck crab-free. Whisker had never seen anyone fight with so much speed and precision – strike, block, pivot, counter, lunge, step, guard, grapple. Each move led seamlessly into the next like a perfectly choreographed dance.

'Wow!' he gasped in awe.

'Eyes on the job, blue eyes!' Horace shouted, knocking a sneaky crab from the mainsail.

'S-sorry,' Whisker stammered. 'I was learning some new moves.'

Horace gave him a sly grin. 'Sure you were … now lend me a paw to raise the anchor.'

It took the combined strength of Horace, Whisker and the two mice to heave the heavy anchor onto the deck. It was officially Fred's job, but his paws were busy fighting two dozen crabs at the bow of the boat.

With the anchor raised and the sails unfurled, the *Apple*

Pie moved swiftly through the waves.

'Where am I headed?' Mr Tribble called from the helm.

'Away from these cursed commandos!' the Captain barked. 'Just watch out for shipwrecks and shallow water!'

Mr Tribble gave the wheel a hard spin and the *Apple Pie* jerked violently to the left. Half a dozen crabs tumbled overboard.

'Turn starboard!' Horace shouted. 'We're headed for a wreck!'

Mr Tribble swung the wheel frantically in the opposite direction.

'Port!' Pete hollered. 'You're steering into the sandbar!'

'I'm a teacher, not a navigator!' Mr Tribble shrieked, spinning the wheel chaotically from side to side.

'Just turn the wheel *gently*!' Pete spluttered.

Mr Tribble took a deep breath, steadied himself and delicately turned the wheel.

The attacking crabs thinned out and swimmers fell by the wayside as the *Apple Pie* continued through the early morning obstacle course of water-logged hulls and sunken cargo ships. Whisker looked down from his position on the rigging to see the last handful of clawed commandos standing in the corner of the deck.

'They're mine!' Horace cried, rushing forward.

Ruby appeared out of nowhere and stepped in his way.

'Ladies first!' she smirked.

'That's not fair!' Horace protested. 'You've got *two* swords and you always get more crabs.'

'Stop complaining!' Ruby snapped. '*You* had a head start.'

'Whatever happened to sharing?' Pete groaned from across the deck.

As Ruby and Horace continued bickering, the huge

shape of Fred emerged behind them. The remaining crabs took one look at the giant and leapt overboard.

'Putrid pastries!' Horace huffed in annoyance. 'Two more crabs and I would have reached thirty.'

'What a shame,' Ruby hissed. 'One more and I would have had *fifty*!'

Horace ignored her and turned to Fred. 'How many big fella? Eighty? Ninety?'

'Ten,' Fred replied with a baffled shrug.

Ruby grinned triumphantly at Horace and pranced down the stairs to hunt for unwanted passengers below. The remaining crew assembled at the helm. Mr Tribble looked extremely relieved when Pete offered to take the wheel.

'It's much harder than it looks,' he admitted.

'So what did our new friends want?' the Captain asked quietly. 'They didn't mention *you-know-what* did they?'

'The Forgotten Map?' Whisker gasped. 'No ...'

It had only been a few hours since Whisker's daring map-retrieval mission (he still stank of perfume from his flamboyant getaway from Madam Pearl's boutique shop) and the last thing he wanted was for the map to fall into the claws of the Aladryan Navy.

'There's nothing to worry about, Captain,' Horace said confidently. 'Those hard-headed coral crunchers wouldn't know the difference between a treasure map and a piece of toilet paper!'

'Then perhaps their attack was connected to last night's raid?' the Captain wondered.

'You mean *today's* raid,' Pete muttered, pointing a bony finger out to sea. 'The note we intercepted mentioned a blockade of warships to the west, and we've just sailed out

19

of our only safe haven!'

The Captain stroked his chin thoughtfully. 'I hadn't intended on leaving Shipwreck Sandbar until the blockade had disbanded on Saturday morning. But then again, no Claw-of-War would venture within firing range of the sandbar – the water is far too shallow. If we head due-south through the remaining wrecks, we may escape unseen …'

'And then what?' Pete said sceptically. 'Drop in for a slice of pie on Prison Island?'

Horace gave Pete a prod with his hook. 'Lighten up, grumpy bones! If we turn west *before* we reach Prison Island, we'll be on a direct course for the Island of Kings – where the missing key awaits us!'

'You make it sound so easy, Horace,' Pete muttered. 'I'll wager my breakfast there's a Claw-of-War lurking beyond the last wreck.'

'I'll accept your wager,' Horace said eagerly. 'If the coast is clear, I'm a well fed rat!'

'You'll be a well *starved* rat …' Pete sniggered under his breath.

Pete turned the *Apple Pie* to the south and Whisker helped the mice adjust the sails. Horace and Fred busied themselves removing broken crab claws and other debris from the deck. Ruby soon emerged at the top of the stairs and stood frowning at the multitude of scratch marks left by the crabs.

'Anything to report, my dear?' the Captain asked with interest.

'No, Uncle,' she replied, her expression lightening. 'I found your cabin untouched and the Forgotten Map still hidden in the top drawer.'

Whisker let out a sigh of relief. Legend foretold that the

Forgotten Map led to a mysterious treasure of great power on the Island of Destiny. It was Whisker's silent hope that the treasure would bring back his parents and sister, who disappeared in their little red boat on the night he was washed overboard in the cyclone. Whisker clung to the belief they were still alive …

His thoughts were interrupted by an excited cry from Horace: 'Argh me pastries! Last wreck to our starboard side! Put the kettle on, Fred!'

'Hold your rat's tails,' Pete said warily. 'I think the Captain should take a look at this.'

The Captain clambered up to the helm and raised a short telescope to his eye. Horace and Whisker scurried after him. Pete stood motionless behind the wheel, looking queasy.

'So?' Horace squeaked, tugging the Captain's sleeve. 'Who misses breakfast?'

The Captain lowered the telescope. 'I'm afraid you *both* do.'

'What?' Horace gasped, turning a sickly shade of green.

'There's no Claw-of-War,' the Captain elaborated, 'but the coast is definitely *not* clear.'

'S-s-so what's out there?' Whisker stammered, suddenly feeling as ill as the others.

'I'll give you a hint,' the Captain said, deadpan. 'They smell like fish, but they can't stand water …'

TWO

Out of the crab pot ...

There was an old Pie Rat saying that cats and rats got along like naked flames and barrels of gunpowder – explosively! As Whisker watched the armour-plated vessel of the Cat Fish racing towards him, he knew the comparison was frightfully accurate – the *Silver Sardine* was notorious for firing flaming fur-balls!

'Simple Simon save us,' Pete groaned in desperation. 'They're coming for the map!'

'I thought Whisker blew up their rust-bucket boat last night,' Horace said, confused.

The Captain extended his telescope for a closer look.

'The *Silver Sardine* is definitely afloat,' he said. 'Though it appears her cannons are still out of action.'

'Small consolation,' Pete muttered. '*We're* out of cannon-pies!'

Mr Tribble raised a trembling paw. 'Might I suggest we take our chances with the shipwrecks, Captain? At least we won't be eaten.'

The Captain swung his telescope towards the sandbar and let out an agitated groan. 'Ratbeard be kind! The Blue Claw are back for round two. The water is teeming with them!'

Pete stamped his pencil in frustration. 'Confounded crabs! Conniving cats! Can't we find an easier enemy?'

'What are our other options?' the Captain asked, attempting to remain calm.

Ruby drew both swords and voiced her opinion with a cry of 'fight!' The Captain politely shook his head and turned expectantly to Whisker.

Since his dramatic rescue, Whisker had become the official *go-to rat* in dangerous situations. He'd saved the crew more than once with his desperate decision making and last-minute escape plans.

'Err ... well,' he mumbled, beginning a process of elimination. 'We can't sail north while the crabs occupy the sandbar, and we can't sail east with the mainland in the way. The *Silver Sardine* is blocking our southern escape route ... but we could take our chances to the west and try to outsail them ...'

'What about the blockade?' Pete interrupted.

The crew looked nervously at Whisker. Whisker knew his plan was risky, but less risk than facing the cats.

'If we encounter a blockade,' he replied, 'the Cat Fish are in as much trouble as we are!'

With a hesitant nod of heads, the *Apple Pie* turned west. Immediately, the *Silver Sardine* changed course and the pursuit was on.

Shipwreck Sandbar disappeared from sight as the two ships ploughed through the ocean. The *Apple Pie* had the up-wind advantage and a favourable breeze from the north-east kept her sails full. The *Silver Sardine*, however, carried an extra sail. The Pie Rats worked hard to maintain their speed but it wasn't long before the Cat Fish began gaining ground.

The specks of distant ships appeared on the horizon and the Captain handed Whisker the telescope, with a mumble of 'Now what?'

Whisker raised the telescope to his eye and peered through. His vision filled with the ominous shapes of warships, curving in a wide arc across the sea. He turned the telescope to the *Silver Sardine*. Six cats stood on the deck, slicing cheese knives through the air in readiness.

Whisker gulped in terror. On an empty stomach, and with very little sleep, the prospect of arrest was far easier to swallow than a mid-sea massacre. As his trembling paws lowered the telescope, he felt his mind retreating into the calm world of his memories.

He closed his eyes. Distant recollections floated in and out of his mind as he searched for an answer: *What should I do?* He'd first experienced this strange phenomenon when he was sinking in the Cyclone Sea. His memories had found him an answer and the answer had saved his life.

Whisker focused his thoughts. Past memories turned to recent events. Images became clearer ...

He was on the *Apple Pie*. A waterlogged mouse wearing thick glasses climbed aboard. In his paws he clutched a pile of precious books wrapped up in a school flag ...

Whisker opened his eyes. The Cat Fish showed no signs of altering their course.

'Good,' he mumbled. 'Sometimes it pays to have enemies.'
'What's that?' the Captain asked expectantly.
A mischievous grin spread across Whisker's face.
'Captain,' he said, 'how would you feel about giving the

Apple Pie a little makeover?'

The Captain flashed Whisker a puzzled expression. 'Are you sure that's not the perfume talking?'

Whisker gave himself a quick sniff. The scent of roses and cherry blossoms filled his nose.

'N-no, Captain,' he replied.

'Very well,' the Captain sighed. 'I don't know what goes through that crazy circus head of yours, Whisker, but if it gets us out alive, get beautifying!'

'LISTEN UP CREW!' the Captain bellowed across the deck. 'Whisker has a plan! Do exactly what he asks – no questions. That means you, Horace!'

'Yeah, yeah,' Horace muttered back. 'I may be a chatterbox, but I do know when to keep my mouth sh ...'

'ZIP IT!' the Captain roared.

Horace stuck his hook in his mouth and Whisker wasted no time in rattling off a peculiar list of requests.

'First, I need a spare set of sails – the brighter, the better; plus any ribbons, scarves or bunting you can find. Second, I require Pete's collection of books to be stacked on the deck and all cannons and scissor swords hidden away. Third, I need Ruby and Horace to swap clothes with Emmie and Eaton. And finally, I need Mr Tribble's school flag flying up there!' He thrust his finger in the direction of the foremast.

The crew stared back in bewilderment. Not even Horace dared to ask *why?*

With two sharp claps from the Captain, the crew leapt into action. They swarmed below, raiding the cargo hold, closing cannon hatches and turning Pete's cabin inside out. In minutes the deck was covered with flowing fabric and piles of books.

Whisker surveyed the ship. In the centre of the deck, Ruby fossicked through a pile of spare sails. Nearby, Horace raised the Oakbridge school flag up the mast.

'I can barely move in this getup!' Horace complained, unbuttoning Eaton's school blazer with his hook.

'Try cutting back on the pies,' Ruby muttered.

'That's hardly fair,' Horace whined. 'I've already missed breakfast!'

Ruby held up a red and green sail.

'What about this one, Whisker?' she asked. 'It's a giant tomato.'

Whisker walked over for a closer look. Ruby fidgeted awkwardly in Emmie's maroon blazer, but stopped when she realised Whisker was approaching.

'School was never my thing,' she said awkwardly. 'They didn't teach sword fighting. Besides, no one could possibly look good in one of these!'

'Oh,' Whisker replied. 'I think you look, um … well … th-the colour suits you.'

Ruby looked away in embarrassment. Whisker felt his cheeks turning a brighter shade of red than the tomato sail.

Trying to act normal, Ruby pointed to another sail. 'There's a matching carrot if you want to use it. I prefer the eagle sail, but it's much too large for the masts.'

'H-healthy eating,' Whisker stammered, saying the first thing that came into his head. 'Tomatoes and carrots. Yes, that's what we're after…'

Horace's ears pricked up. 'Healthy eating? Are you having a go at me, too?'

Whisker knew he had to stay focused.

'I-I have to check on the others,' he said, darting off.

The rest of the crew were doing exactly what Whisker

had requested. Eaton and Emmie (dressed as miniature versions of Horace and Ruby) dangled from the front of the boat, draping the Mer-Mouse figurehead with colourful scarves. Fred and Smudge hung a line of blue bunting between the masts while Pete and Mr Tribble stacked neat piles of books on the deck. There wasn't a cannon or scissor sword in sight. As the final vegetable sail was raised, Whisker glanced over his shoulder to see the *Silver Sardine* rapidly approaching.

'Horace to the wheel!' he ordered. 'Ruby and the twins to the sails and the rest of the rats in the navigation room, NOW!'

'What about me?' Mr Tribble asked apprehensively.

'I have a special job for you,' Whisker said, handing Mr Tribble a white flag. 'Wave this in the air and act like a school teacher escaping from a ship of hungry cats!'

Four rats and a blowfly crouched in a clutter of sails in a corner of the navigation room.

'Tell me again,' Fred said, untangling himself from the eagle sail. 'Why are we hiding in here?'

'Because I'm too bony for a school boy and you're too scary for a teacher!' Pete replied impatiently.

Smudge raised four arms in the air as if to say, *and I'm too unhygienic for a classroom pet!*

'Oh – right,' Fred mumbled.

'Just keep your eye on those cats and tell us if they're up to anything,' the Captain instructed.

Fred closed his mouth and stared out the rear window. The Captain crept to the front of the room, raising his telescope to a pane of glass in the door.

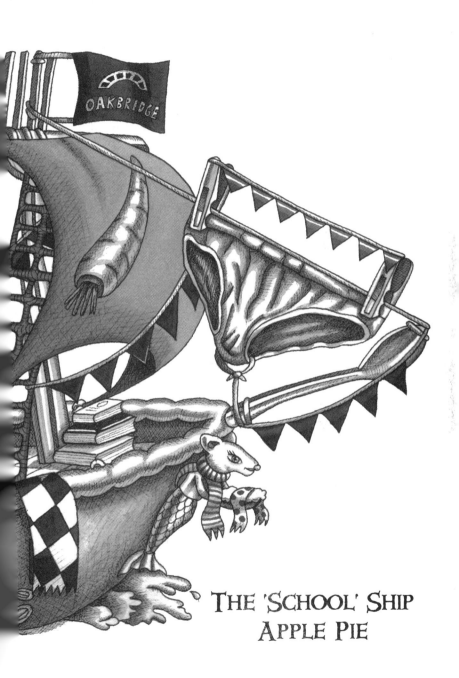

THE 'SCHOOL' SHIP
APPLE PIE

'We're almost within firing range of the warships,' the Captain said. 'We should expect the first round of volcanic rocks any minute.'

'That'll put a chink in the cats' armour!' Pete smirked.

'Or a big hole in *our* boat,' Whisker added, hoping desperately the crabs were as easily fooled as they'd been in the past.

'Um, sorry to interrupt,' Fred said slowly. 'But I think the cats are up to something.'

The rats rushed over to Fred and peered out the rear window. The *Silver Sardine* was now only a stone's throw away. They watched as the shaggy shape of Furious Fur appeared at the bow of the boat, clutching a pronged metal object attached to a rope.

'Murderous mayhem!' Pete cried frantically. 'He's got a grappling hook!'

The Captain seized the closest scissor sword and whacked the ceiling, roaring, 'PORT SIDE ON THE DOUBLE!'

Whisker heard a muffled cry from Horace and the *Apple Pie* suddenly lurched to its left. A moment later, the grappling hook hurtled past the window, narrowly missing the hull, and splashed harmlessly into the water on the starboard side of the ship.

Furious Fur hissed in anger and slashed his claws through the air. The terrifying orange and black figure of Captain Sabre came into view beside him. Together, the two cats heaved the soggy rope onto the deck.

'They'll get us next time!' Pete hollered. 'And then we're brunch!'

As the grappling hook rose from the surface of the water and Sabre prepared to swing, Whisker hoped Pete was wrong.

With a deafening *BOOM! BOOM! BOOM!* a chorus of exploding cannons filled the air. To Whisker, the sound was sweeter than birds chirping on a spring afternoon.

With deadly speed and precision, a dozen jagged missiles pounded the metal hull of the *Silver Sardine*. Sabre was thrown backwards into Furious Fur and together the two cats landed in a sprawling heap on the deck. There was a defeated hiss of 'RETREAT!' and the chase was over. When the second wave of projectiles arrived, the Cat Fish were already racing away.

Jubilant rejoicing filled the deck of the *Apple Pie*. Cries of 'We're saved!' and 'Lady Luck is with us!' echoed through the salty air. The celebration inside the navigation room was far more restrained.

'What happens next?' Pete asked, in his usual negative tone.

'We sail through the blockade and escape,' Whisker replied, sounding far more confident than he felt. 'The warships are here to stop smugglers, not traumatised school students.'

'Just because we *look* like a ship of traumatised school students ...' Pete said doubtfully.

No one responded. It was clearly a matter of *wait and see*.

Horace poked his head through the doorway.

'Who died?' he said, staring at the long faces.

'Not *you*,' Pete snarled. 'That would be a joyous occasion.'

'Quiet!' the Captain hissed. 'Why are you here, Horace?'

'I've come to ask Fred for recess,' Horace answered. 'The whole class is starving!'

'Aren't you supposed to be steering the ship?' the

Captain asked suspiciously.

'Don't worry,' Horace said in a relaxed tone. 'Mr Tribble's covering for me.'

'Mr Tribble!' Pete spluttered. 'The plan was to sail *through* the blockade, not crash into it!'

The horrified look on Horace's face told the rats that recess could wait. He kicked the door open and darted outside. Whisker stared through the open doorway. Towering over the deck was the most enormous ship he had ever seen. Its giant claw-shaped battering ram protruded from its bow, its four masts extended high into the air and its twelve billowing sails blocked out the sun. It was a monstrous Claw-of-War, and it was on a collision course with the *Apple Pie*.

Mr Tribble let out a startled cry and the crew took evasive action. Ruby and the twins tugged frantically at ropes in a desperate attempt to collapse the sails. Horace seized the wheel and spun the ship in a tight arc through the water. Whisker grabbed the door frame to steady himself as the port side of the *Apple Pie* lurched towards the starboard side of the warship. An entire battalion of crabs gasped as the two ships scraped past each other with a piercing screech of timber.

For a moment the ships were locked in a grinding embrace, but with the jolt of a passing wave, they sprang apart and the collision was over. Whisker staggered backwards through the doorway, pulling the door shut behind him. With the click of the latch, there was silence.

He cautiously pressed his nose against the glass. Outside, six hundred beady eyes stared transfixed at Horace. Whisker reached for a scissor sword, expecting the crabs to hurl themselves aboard at any moment, but not one of them twitched. The uncanny silence continued until a small voice broke the stillness.

'Stupid kid!' piped a crab. 'You nearly killed us all!'

'You're sailing on the wrong side of the sea!' scolded another.

'That's a week of detention!' cried a third.

'The repairs are coming out of your pocket money!' snapped a fourth.

Horace responded with a string of apologies: 'Whoops … terribly sorry … it's entirely my fault … yes, we're insured … no, it won't happen again … of course I'm not sailing under the influence … I know, I know. I should never let a history teacher behind the wheel – it's all theory with them …'

The crabs appeared convinced that Horace was in fact an inexperienced schoolboy and the mice were preschoolers in fancy dress, and let them off with a stern warning. It didn't stop the crabs hurling a claw-full of school insults as the *Apple Pie* drifted past.

'Oakbridge Smokebridge!' they chanted. 'Crab Valley High rules!'

'You've all got head lice!'

'Hey smarty pants. What's four minus four?'

'I dunno …?'

'A mouse with no legs!'

'Ha, ha, that's a good one …'

The chuckling voices drifted away in the wind and the Pie Rats sailed right through the blockade. Soon nothing lay between the bow of the *Apple Pie* and the open sea. Four rats and a blowfly let out a collective sigh of relief.

'Well, that went well,' Pete muttered sarcastically. 'So much for laying low in the Shipwreck Sea, enjoying a relaxing day off. Three close encounters and it's not even midday. Call me paranoid but I swear something's amiss.'

'You may be right, Pete,' the Captain added gravely. 'The Cat Fish have found us twice in as many days, which leads me to believe they know more about our quest than we first realised.'

'Rat Bait!' Pete hissed, stamping his pencil leg. 'I've said it once and I'll say it again: the dirty scoundrel's double-crossed us. He's ratted us out, I tell you!'

'But Rat Bait despises the Cat Fish as much as we do,' Whisker piped up. 'I saw how he acted on Sea Shanty Island when Sabre demanded the map. There's no way he'd cut a deal with a bloodthirsty cat.'

Pete let out a condescending snort. 'Don't underestimate the power of riches, young Whisker – especially when it comes to a bounty of Cat Fish silver. Rat Bait wouldn't be the first Pie Rat captain to do the dirty on his fellow rats –' He stopped.

The Captain shot him a look of pure disgust. 'My father has nothing to do with this, Pete.'

'Sorry, Captain,' Pete muttered, shrinking into the shadows. 'I won't mention him again.'

'Good,' the Captain snapped. 'Because right now we have more to worry about than a couple of rotten rats.' He pointed a shaky finger through the doorway. 'If you hadn't noticed, that wasn't just a routine blockade we passed through. It was nothing short of a fully-armed battle formation. Every ship was equipped with extra cannons and additional troops. At an estimate, three quarters of the entire Aladryan navy was assembled out there. I have no doubt that something big is brewing – something that goes beyond the raids, beyond the arrests and beyond the attempts to stop the Pirate Cup!'

'Oh dear!' Fred gasped, his enormous eye spinning in manic circles. 'Oh double dear!'

'B-but what are they preparing for?' Whisker asked fearfully.

'I'm not sure,' the Captain said, walking towards the door. 'But there's more to this than meets the eye and I, for one, have no intention of sticking around to find out!' He burst onto the deck, closely followed by Whisker and the rest of the anxious crew.

'Is it lunch time yet, Captain?' Horace moaned from the helm. 'We couldn't possibly fit any more danger into one morning.'

The Captain clambered up the stairs without a response, his brow deeply furrowed.

'Oh, come on,' Horace pleaded. 'We're in the clear and I'm famished!'

Whisker was about to agree that even Horace deserved a large slice of pie, following their narrow escape, when he remembered a piece of advice passed down from his great-grandfather Anso: *If it appears too good to be true, it probably is too good to be true!'* Whisker took this to mean: Stop. Take a careful look around – and prepare to panic!

Whisker stopped and looked around. Mr Tribble did the panicking.

'Th-Th-Thunderclaw!' he stuttered. '*D-D-Dreadnaught*! B-b-behind us!'

Whisker's eyes grew wide. The blockade of ships lay far to the east. One ship, however, had broken from the fleet and was charging through the water towards them. Its colossal size made the other warships look like matchstick models. It was a four-masted monstrosity and it needed no introduction.

THE
DREADNAUGHT

Every teacher, student, pirate, blowfly and circus rat on the Isle of Aladrya knew what it was. It was the blue jewel of the navy. It was the pride of the fleet. It was the pirate crusher, the smuggler smasher. Captained by the General of the navy himself, it was a destroyer in a class of its own. It was the mighty *Dreadnaught*!

The sight of the terrifying ship told Whisker one thing: General Thunderclaw, the most feared officer on the seas, wanted them dead. He was rarely outsmarted and he never made arrests.

The Captain removed his hat like a mourner at a funeral.

'Well, that spoils everything,' he sighed. 'We've bitten off more than we can chew this time. Thunderclaw's no fool. If he's after us, he's on to us.'

Whisker's tail dropped to the deck.

'Sorry,' he mumbled, pointing at the jib sail. 'I should have removed the red underpants.'

'It's no one's fault, Whisker,' the Captain assured him. 'Your plan was exceptional.' He raised his telescope and assessed the situation.

'Can we fight them?' Ruby asked, hopefully.

'Suicide,' the Captain said coldly. 'The *Dreadnaught*, like the rest of the fleet, is carrying a reinforced troop numbers – four hundred crabs, at least. She's sitting low in the water, which tells me she's armed with enough volcanic rocks to sink us six times over! She'll either ram us from behind or blast us to bits from the side.'

'Oh my!' Mr Tribble gasped. 'Surely we can outrun her?'

'Slim chance,' the Captain replied. 'She may be overloaded, but she's fully rigged with twelve sails. The *Apple Pie* has three, including the underpants. Spare sails aren't much good without masts.'

'Perhaps we could surrender?' Horace said tentatively.

'That option's long gone!' Pete sniffled.

'But – but – there must be *something* we can do,' Mr Tribble pleaded in desperation.

The Captain shook his head in defeat and took his place behind the wheel. Mr Tribble put his arms around the mice, Smudge hid behind a pile of books, Pete scribbled *RIP: Rest in Pies* on the deck and the others stared hopelessly up at the sky.

The clouds overhead were fluffy and white. Whisker wished they were heavy and black – storms clouds had saved them before.

Fred pointed high into the air.

'If only we could fly like those birds,' he said dreamily. 'They're much faster than our ship.'

'Well, we can't!' Pete quibbled. 'We don't have any wings! Besides, the wind is stronger up there, so the lazy creatures are getting a free ride.'

'Birds aren't lazy,' Fred said defensively. 'A falcon once spent a whole hour trying to catch me for its dinner before I beat it off with a stick.'

'Are you sure it was a real bird and not that ridiculous eagle sail flapping around in the navigation room?' Pete said spitefully.

Fred's ears drooped. Whisker's tail shot straight into the air – *of course!*

He looked at the sky. He looked at the navigation room. He looked at Ruby. Her green eye sparkled back at him. She knew what he was thinking.

'You get the eagle,' she said excitedly, 'and I'll get the rope!' She rushed over to Fred and gave him a big kiss on the cheek. 'You're a genius, Fred!'

Fred gave Ruby a confused smile. Pete screwed up his nose.

'Hey!' Horace exclaimed. 'I've never got a kiss for a brilliant suggestion before.'

Ruby rolled her eye. 'I'd hardly call your suggestions brilliant, Horace!'

'Well, what about Whisker?' Horace asked audaciously. 'He has brilliant ideas *all* the time.'

Whisker felt his cheeks ripen to a triple-strength tomato red.

'Just-just give Whisker a hand with the eagle!' Ruby spluttered. 'Or you'll both be kissing crabs!'

THREE

Let's go Fly a Kite

Things moved quickly when Ruby took control. She was impatient, but she was efficient. As the ship's boatswain, the deck was her domain.

'Find me four strong fixing points on the bulwark,' she barked. 'And bring me every rope that's not holding up a sail. Who's good at tying knots?'

'Not me,' Horace replied, holding up his hook. 'Ask the mice. They've got small fingers!'

Ruby pointed at Mr Tribble. 'Give me your best *Double Fisherman's* knot, pronto!'

Mr Tribble gave Ruby a timid salute and, with Eaton and Emmie's assistance, began tying short lengths of rope together. Fred reinforced the fixing points with saucepan handles, while Whisker and Horace dragged the eagle sail onto the deck. Soon four enormous lengths of rope were attached to the corners of the sail. The Pie Rats had their kite sail!

The *Dreadnaught* continued its swift approach, halving its distance to the *Apple Pie* in a few short minutes.

'I need four strong teams to feed the rope through the fixing points,' Ruby snapped, 'and a volunteer to launch the eagle. Whisker! Up the mast!'

Whisker was accustomed to Ruby's demands, so without protest he wrapped his tail around the sail and scampered up the rigging. The rest of the crew took their positions on the ropes.

'Swing us around so we're running downwind,' Ruby shouted to the Captain.

'Aye, aye, my dear,' the Captain cried, with a vigorous turn of the wheel.

Whisker felt a strong gust of wind on his back as he reached the top of the foremast. Twisting his tail around the rigging to steady himself, he grasped the sail in both paws and shouted down to the waiting crew, 'Let her out!'

The crew fed the ropes through the fixing points and the kite sail expanded with air, rising steadily upwards. Whisker held on with all his might until he was certain it had enough lift and released his grip. The golden eagle soared majestically into the sky.

On any other day, Whisker would have raised his arms to the heavens and shouted in triumph. But on any other day, there wasn't a *Dreadnaught* on his tail.

He glanced over his shoulder. The giant ship had shifted to a port side position in readiness for a broadside cannon attack.

'Get down from there, Whisker!' the Captain shouted with urgency. 'The volcano is about to erupt!'

Whisker saw the flashes before he heard the booms. Half a dozen volcanic rocks hurtled through the air. He grabbed the mast with both paws and squeezed his eyes shut.

Terrified, he waited for the impact.

SPLASH!

SPLASH!

SPLASH!
SPLASH!
SPLASH!
… SPLASH!
Silence.

Whisker squinted through one eye – just to make sure he hadn't mistaken a splash for a crash.

'Not even close,' Horace shouted into the wind. 'So long, snappers!'

Whisker was halfway down the rigging when the cannons exploded again. This time he kept his eyes open. There was nothing to fear. The eagle was airborne and the Pie Rats were flying without wings.

One-and-three-quarter potato pies later, Whisker rubbed his bulging belly and wiped the last crumb from his cheek. He couldn't remember a more enjoyable lunch – even if it was just plain potato pie. Horace and Pete sat next to him, still munching away and reflecting on their good fortune.

While the others finished their pies, Whisker absentmindedly fiddled with the gold anchor pendant around his neck, a gift from his parents. Some called it a lucky charm. To Whisker, it was a symbol of hope.

Horace watched him closely.

'There's *ordinary* luck,' Horace mumbled between mouthfuls, 'and then there's *how on earth did we survive that* luck.'

'I don't believe in luck,' Pete said scathingly. 'I believe in rules.'

As the Quartermaster of the ship, Pete was a stickler for rules, especially when it came to the Pie Rat code, a six hundred page book in his possession. Whisker followed *most* of the rules, though he still had to learn how to fight.

'It's simple logic,' Pete argued. 'By following the code, we're best equipped for whatever dangers come our way. Luck has nothing to do with it.'

'Don't spoil the moment with your logic talk!' Horace spluttered, spraying bits of potato all over the table. 'Don't you see? The power of the map is at work!'

Pete screwed up his nose. 'The map has no power, you brainless barnacle. The *treasure* has the power! And at this rate, we'll all be dead before we find the blasted key!'

'The King's Key!' Horace exclaimed. 'Do you think it's lucky, too?'

'No, I don't!' Pete snapped. 'That infuriating riddle said nothing about luck.'

'Why don't we take another look?' Horace said in a low voice. 'We know where the map is hidden ...'

Whisker felt a sudden surge of excitement race through his tail.

Pete eyed Whisker and Horace cautiously.

'Alright,' he agreed. 'There's no harm in looking, and we've got plenty of time before we're on eagle duty.' He stood up to go. 'There's one condition, Horace: finish eating first. We don't want the Island of Destiny looking like *Potato Pie Island*!'

While Horace cleaned his teeth with an old scrubbing brush from the galley, Whisker wiped the table clean of crumbs and potato slobber. Pete returned with the Forgotten Map in one paw and a map of the Crescent Sea in the other.

As Pete unrolled the maps, Ruby walked in with a tray

of empty pie platters. She took one look at the three rats and hurriedly plonked the tray on the nearest serving bench.

'Secret boy's business,' she muttered, turning to go.

'H-how's the eagle?' Whisker asked, trying to strike up a conversation.

Ruby took the question as her invitation to stay and hastily pulled up a chair.

'The eagle's flying high,' she said proudly. 'Mr Tribble and the twins have things under control.' She shot a quick glance at Horace. 'It's nice to have crew members who do what they're told for a change!'

Horace shook his hook at her. 'We sank their boat with a flying pie; of course they're going to cooperate!'

Ruby shrugged and continued, 'Sea Shanty Island is coming up on our starboard side. The Captain thinks it's wise to continue to the Island of Kings while we still have the wind.'

Pete nodded his approval. 'Thunderclaw won't give up easily, even if he is miles behind us. He'll expect to find us cowering in fear on Sea Shanty Island. He'll be bitterly disappointed!'

The four rats grinned with satisfaction and turned their attention to the Forgotten Map.

'So, what do we know about this missing key?' Pete asked curiously.

'We know what it looks like, for a start,' Horace said, stating the obvious. 'The hole in the map is a dead giveaway!'

Pete snorted. 'Anything *besides* the fact that the key looks like a key?'

Horace shrugged and read out the mysterious riddle:

45

The Island of Destiny
Directly north-north-west of Drumstick Island

My key is not found in the ground.
It moves through air without a sound.
A treasure for a rich king's throne,
its guard appears as leaves and stone.

Dark and Treacherous your voyage may be,
keep Hope in your sights as you pass through the Sea.
Uncover the key and enlighten your mind,
but wisdom is found in the shadows behind.

Mt
Mobziw

Mt
Moochup

Treacherous
Sea

Whisker ran his finger over the first verse of the riddle, recalling Mr Tribble's interpretation of the words.

'The King's Key is believed to be hanging in the throne tower of the ruined citadel on the Island of Kings,' he explained. 'The key is guarded by leafy vines and high stone walls.' He looked back at the map. 'The second verse is also relevant: *Uncover the key and enlighten your mind*, though I doubt we'll know what that means until we've located the key.'

'What about the last line?' Horace said puzzled. '... *wisdom is found in the shadows behind*. Is that telling us to learn from the bad things that happen along the way?'

'Always the optimist, aren't you, Horace?' Pete taunted. 'I hate to admit it, but for once you could be right!'

Horace beamed with pride.

'How 'bout that, Ruby,' he said, pointing to his cheek.

Ruby responded with a well-placed slap across his face, knocking Horace off his chair.

Dazedly, he staggered back to his seat, muttering, 'That's *not* what I had in mind ...'

Chuckling to herself, Ruby turned her attention to the map of the Crescent Sea.

'This is our current course,' she said, moving her finger from Sea Shanty Island to the Island of Kings. 'Tribble believes there's an overgrown track that follows the eastern river to the mountain citadel.'

'The Eastern River estuary is a risky place to anchor,' Pete said sceptically. 'We can't sail upstream, and the *Apple Pie* will be in full view of any passing ships.'

'Exactly,' Ruby agreed. 'That's why we should anchor here.' She pointed to the mouth of a passage, north of the river. 'We can cut through the marsh and cross the river

48

at Silver Falls. From there, we can join the main track and take the bridge over the ravine. It's a shorter route and the *Apple Pie* will be well concealed by the mangroves.'

Whisker looked carefully at the map.

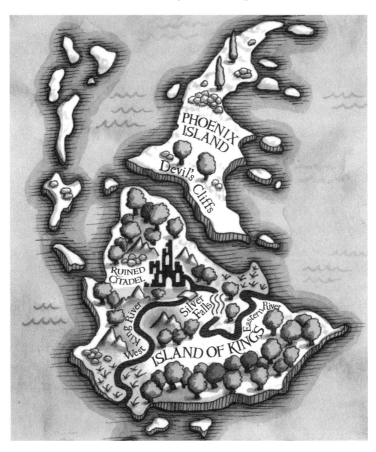

'Why are the cliffs above the passage called Devil's Cliffs?' he asked anxiously.

'Because devils live there,' Pete sniffled.

'Devils!' Whisker gasped. 'Horned beasts with pitchforks and spiky tails?'

'Not those kind of devils,' Horace groaned, rubbing his swollen cheek. 'Tasmanian devils! You know, nasty marsupials that enjoy hurling rocks at passing ships.'

'Oh,' Whisker said, unsure if he should be relieved or even more anxious.

'Don't worry,' Horace reassured him. 'They live on the neighbouring island and only attack ships that sail *through* the passage!'

Whisker hoped Horace was right. There were enough dangers to worry about without adding rock-throwing devils to the list.

The eagle stayed airborne until the early evening when the wind changed direction and darkness crept in. The Pie Rats hauled the giant sail onto the deck and, with two vegetable sails and a pair of red underpants, they continued sailing through the night. The crew took turns monitoring the sails and keeping lookout. It was a relief to all when dawn arrived with no sign of General Thunderclaw and no sightings of the Cat Fish.

The sun rose in the east, and the Island of Kings appeared in the west. Bathed in morning light, the glorious green jungle stretched high into the mountains. Misty patches of cloud clung to the canopy of dense trees. To the north of the island, the foreboding shapes of Devil's Cliffs rose from the ocean like the walls of a great canyon. Mangroves and mudflats covered the southern shore of the passage. Beyond the mangroves, a grassy marsh extended to the foot of the jungle. Silently, the *Apple Pie* slipped into the passage and anchored out of sight.

While the sun was still low, the Captain gathered the

sleepy crew onto the deck. It took a few firm jabs in the backside from Pete's pencil to fully awaken Horace, but when he was finally standing to attention, the Captain began.

'The perilous jungle lies before us. Our mission to retrieve the key will be challenging, to say the least. Due to the unique dangers of the island, Mr Tribble has offered to act as our official guide. He has extensive knowledge of its flora and fauna and understands its complex history.'

Mr Tribble nodded timidly and fumbled with a button on his chequered waist coat.

'Not exactly *Survival Mouse*, is he?' Horace whispered to Whisker.

The Captain shot Horace an unimpressed look. 'Crew members who do not wish to join us are free to remain on the *Apple Pie* in readiness for a quick escape, should our whereabouts be discovered. Volunteers for the expedition, please step forward now.'

Whisker, Ruby and Horace took a step towards the Captain. Smudge flew in a circle around the Captain's head and settled on his shoulder. Eaton looked at Mr Tribble and hesitantly stepped forward. The others remained firmly where they stood.

'It looks like I'm stuck with beauty and the beast,' Pete sniffled.

Emmie gave Fred a big hug. 'Don't listen to him, Uncle Fred. We'll have hours of fun baking pies in the galley!'

Fred smiled fondly at her. Pete screwed up his nose in disapproval.

'What's Pete got to complain about?' Horace muttered to Whisker. 'He's got two personal chefs and not a single leech, strangling vine or rat-eating plant to contend with!'

Whisker's tail went limp. He'd forgotten about the rat-eating plants. Volunteering suddenly seemed like a bad idea. It was only the thought of finding his family that stopped him rushing below to join the cooking class.

The Captain went on, 'Members of our expedition are required to carry essential survival items. Please collect any items you wish to include and place them on the deck immediately.'

'Aye, aye, Captain,' cheered the volunteers.

Whisker made his way down the stairs, forming a list of items in his head: *Number one – a scissor sword. Number two – a hearty fruit pie. Number three …*

'Matches!' he said to himself as he reached the gun deck. 'A Pie Rat can't survive without them.'

He entered the dark space and searched behind a couple of cannons for a matchbox. Unable to locate a single match, he turned his attention to a crate filled with strange looking rocket shapes.

'Apprenticeship graduation fireworks,' he said quietly, picking up a blue rocket. 'Hmm. That's a long way off.'

He tried to remember the seven tests he had to pass before he became a full member of the crew. *Survival, Strength, Strategy, Self-reliance, Sailing, Swords-rat-ship* and *Sacrifice.*

'I've passed two tests,' he thought aloud. '*Survival* and *Strategy* … but they were accidents …'

'They weren't accidents,' whispered a voice from the dark.

Whisker jumped. 'W-who's there?'

'Only me,' Horace whistled, stepping out of the shadows. 'I wouldn't recommend the fireworks. They're a little temperamental in rainforest environments.'

'Err, point taken,' Whisker said, hastily returning the rocket to the crate. 'Have you seen any matches?'

Horace held up two boxes with his hook, keeping his paw hidden behind his back. 'I'm one step ahead of you!'

Whisker looked at him suspiciously. An open crate lay to Horace's right.

'What else have you got?' Whisker asked.

'Oh … nothing,' Horace replied guiltily. 'Just a few *essential* items …'

'A few sticks of Deadly Dynamite you mean!' Whisker exclaimed. 'The Captain would never allow it!'

'Shh,' Horace hissed. 'You're beginning to sound like Pete. The Captain doesn't have to know …'

Whisker was well aware of the trouble the dynamite could get them both into and held his ground.

'Look,' Horace whispered, holding up the sticks. 'They've got extra long fuses, so we'll have plenty of time to run away.' He gave Whisker a pleading look. 'Come on, Whisker. They've saved us before.'

'Alright,' Whisker finally agreed, remembering the exploding pie incident. 'But only a couple …'

'You won't regret it!' Horace said, stuffing two sticks into a backpack.

Whisker sighed. Something told him he would.

Back on the deck, the crew laid out their essential items. There were six boxes of matches, five scissor swords, three water flasks, two fruit pies, a notebook, a small stub of pencil, a coil of rope, a compass, Eaton's mirrored lantern, a bottle of lantern oil, a ball of string, three candy canes and the Forgotten Map rolled up in a canister.

Horace scratched his head with his hook. 'How are candy canes *essential* items?'

Ruby gave him a sour look. 'I thought that was obvious. We tie them together to make a grappling hook, or eat them if we run out of food!'

'Fair enough,' Horace shrugged. 'Speaking of all things sweet, do we have any of Pete's treacle medicine?'

'We're all out,' Pete grumbled. 'Whisker drank it all!'

'Oh yeah,' Horace recalled. 'After that giant spider crab tried to rip his arm off!'

Whisker rubbed his shoulder and winced.

'Come to think of it,' Pete considered, 'you're likely to find the two herbs I need for a new batch while you're frolicking in the jungle. The first herb comes from a large-leafed plant that looks like this –' He hastily sketched the plant on the deck. 'I don't need the leaves, just the dried roots.'

'I'm aware of that species,' Mr Tribble said knowledgeably.

'Good for you,' Pete sniffled. 'Make sure Horace doesn't bring back a bag of shrivelled sweet potatoes by mistake!'

Horace stuck out his tongue.

'The second herb,' Pete continued, ignoring Horace,

'comes from the red fruit of a climbing plant. When the fruit ripens, it pops open like an eyeball. You can't miss it. Bring me the black seeds. Autumn is approaching, so there could be some early ripe fruit.'

'What quantity do you require?' Mr Tribble asked.

'Equal quantities of each dried herb,' Pete stated. 'One to numb the pain and the other for a healing rush of energy. Bring as much as you can carry. With a reckless apprentice on board, I'm sure to run out in no time!'

Whisker considered sticking out *his* tongue but decided that Pete was probably right.

The supplies were packed into calico backpacks and the team of jungle adventurers clambered into the small rowboat. Pete and Emmie waved goodbye from the deck to the out-of-tune chants of, '*Row, row, row your boat*' as Fred ferried the companions to shore.

The quest for the key had begun.

Puddle Mucking

'**M**ud, mud, mud,' Horace moaned. 'Nothing but mud!'

It was low tide and the mangrove-dotted mudflat prevented the rowboat from travelling any further. With a soft bump, the vessel ran aground.

'That will do, Fred,' the Captain said. 'We can walk from here.'

'Squelch through muddy puddles, more like it,' Horace muttered sulkily. 'It's easy for you tall folks, but look at me. I've hardly got the long legs of a flamingo!'

'Or the elegance,' Ruby smirked, as Horace stumbled out of the boat, landing spreadeagled in the mud.

Whisker swung his body over the side of the small vessel. Sticky mud oozed through his toes. Reluctantly he hoisted up his trousers and trudged after Horace. Fred gave the companions a departing grunt and began rowing back to the *Apple Pie*.

The Pie Rats hadn't trekked far when Whisker heard a loud *SPLOOSH* behind him. He whipped his neck around to see a large ripple expanding from the centre of a nearby puddle.

'What was that?' he asked anxiously.

'Probably a bored toadfish,' Horace replied morosely. 'I suspect he's tired of eating mud for breakfast!'

Whisker gazed into the puddle. There was another *SPLOOSH* to his right. He looked up to see a long, scaly creature, twice his size, with a brown, sausage-shaped body twisting in the air. With a sharp flick of its tail, it knocked Horace face-first into the mud before disappearing into the water.

'Jumping jelly cakes!' the Captain exclaimed as Whisker pulled Horace from the mud. 'That's no toad fish!'

'Disgustingly disgusting!' Horace spat. 'Which one of you clowns pushed me in?'

'H-h-he did,' Eaton stammered, pointing to a muddy puddle.

Two black eyes pierced the surface of the water, gazing up at the companions.

'*Periophthalmodon schlosseri*,' Mr Tribble said quietly.

'*Perio*-I'm-gonna-chop-its-ugly-head-off!' Horace roared, reaching for his sword.

'*Periophthalmodon schlosseri*,' Mr Tribble repeated, 'is an amphibious fish that uses its pectoral fins to walk on land. It is commonly known as the *giant mudskipper*.'

'Oh joy!' Horace groaned. 'Yet another creature with the word *giant* in its name. Why can't it be a *miniature* mudskipper for a change?'

Ruby drew both of her swords. 'Can it eat us?'

'It *is* carnivorous ...' Mr Tribble replied.

Smudge wasted no time in scrambling inside the Captain's backpack. There was another *SPLOOSH* and a second mudskipper launched itself from a pond. Its powerful tail thrashed from side to side, its stumpy fins beat the air and its dorsal fin fanned out like the crest of a crazed cockatoo.

'Duck!' the Captain shouted.

The Pie Rats belly-flopped in the mud. The second mudskipper soared over their heads, landing with a SQUELCH on top of the first mudskipper. There was a flurry of fins as the two creatures engaged in a savage wrestling match.

'They're territorial!' Mr Tribble cried. 'We've got to keep moving!'

The rodents scrambled to their feet and took off through the mud. Dozens of mudskippers emerged around them, dragging their slimy bodies from the water. With savage flicks of their tails, they slithered across the mud in pursuit.

'Down on all fours!' the Captain commanded. 'Stay on top of the mud.'

With heads down and front paws scrambling, the Pie Rats raced to escape. They kept to the driest spots, but every puddle they passed contained another waiting menace.

It was fortunate the mudskippers disliked each other more than the trespassers. The moment one got within striking range, another would leap out to protect its territory. Whisker discovered it was safer to run *towards* the mudskippers and jump clear when the wrestling began. It was messy work, but his brazen tactic ensured the mudskippers took out their fury on each other – not on the rodents.

The Pie Rats reached the first mangrove tree and scampered up its slippery trunk, filthy but unscathed. The mudskippers continued to brawl below.

'It's ridiculous,' Horace muttered from an outer branch.

'They're fighting over a patch of mud!'

'Mud to a mudskipper is like a pie to a Pie Rat,' Mr Tribble reasoned. 'Just be thankful they haven't dragged you off to their underwater *mud* burrows.'

'Oh, I'm thankful alright,' Horace gulped, turning his attention back to the fight.

When the mudskipper brawl was over, the companions scurried down the trunk. Fresh attackers joined the pursuit and the Pie Rats dashed towards the next tree. One mangrove at a time, they zigzagged their way through the danger zone. The mud became sandier and the trees grew thicker closer to the shore. Finally, the puddles were little more than moist patches in the hardened mud. Conceding defeat, the mudskippers gave up the chase and retreated to their underwater lairs.

Exhausted, the adventurers collapsed in a dirty heap on the sand and lay panting for several minutes. Not even Horace had the breath to speak.

Whisker sat up and surveyed his surroundings. He was on a sandy strip of earth, separating the mudflat from the freshwater pools of the marsh. A line of shady beach oaks lined the bank. Ruby was already on her feet, impatiently scratching mud from her neck and face.

'Mud is great for your complexion,' Horace remarked, still lying on his back. 'It's a popular beauty treatment back home on Freeforia.'

Ruby glared at him with a wild look in her eye. 'Are you saying I need a beauty treatment, Horace?'

Horace covered his face with his hook.

'No!' he squeaked. 'I was just … saying.'

'Humph!' Ruby snorted and turned away.

Horace lowered his hook and gave Whisker a pleading

stare.

'Go on,' he begged. 'Say something to her.'

'Huh?' Whisker said in confusion.

'So she calms down,' Horace whispered. 'We both know she's worse than a bull with a bee sting when she's angry. And she won't believe a word I say.'

Whisker doubted anything he said would make a difference. It was only recently that Ruby had dropped her major grudge against him. The *Apple Pie* was *her* domain. The Captain was *her* uncle and *he* simply got in her way.

'What should I tell her?' Whisker asked hesitantly.

'Tell her she looks *ravishingly beautiful* even when she's covered in mud,' Horace whispered. 'Girls love hearing that sort of rubbish, especially from handsome young apprentices.'

'I can't say that!' Whisker exclaimed, far louder than he'd intended.

'What can't you say?' the Captain asked, intrigued.

Ruby raised her eye and looked at Whisker. Whisker hoped there was enough mud on his face to hide his reddening cheeks.

'I, err … can't say if mudskippers will be in the marsh,' he lied.

'They won't be,' Mr Tribble said confidently. 'Freshwater crocodiles, perhaps, but definitely no mudskippers.'

Horace flopped backwards into the sand.

'Crocodiles!' he whimpered, 'Can't you give us some good news?'

'Pull yourself together, Horace!' the Captain snapped. 'You haven't stopped whining since we left the boat. Anyone would think you had an acute case of *land-sickness!*'

'I do,' Horace coughed dramatically. 'I can feel the infection spreading. I'm beyond saving … feed me to a crocodile and put me out of my misery…'

The Captain shook his head and dragged Horace to his feet. 'No one's going to feed you to a crocodile, Horace. We'll avoid the pools and stick to the grass. Come on.'

Horace trudged after the Captain, steering well clear of Ruby. She was still cleaning mud off her arms and looked no less angry when Whisker walked past. He plucked up the courage to say something.

'Um, Ruby …' he began.

'What is it?' she said, frowning at the mud.

He tried to find the right words. 'I was just going to say…' He panicked. 'Err … ladies first.'

'Oh,' she said, losing the frown. 'Thanks, *mud boy*. I'm glad there's one gentleman in the crew, even if he does need a good scrub!' She spun on her heel and hurried after the others.

Whisker trailed behind her, scraping mud from his flushed face.

The trek through the marsh was a slow and cautious process. Smudge flew high above the expedition party, guiding them along the grassy banks between pools. More than once the Pie Rats ran into dead ends and more than once they were forced to paddle through shallow water. In places where the reeds grew thick, they clambered up tall stalks and leapt from reed to reed. Despite the challenges of the crossing, the faint croaks of frogs were the only sounds they heard.

As the foot of the jungle drew closer, fallen trees formed

natural bridges, reeds intermingled with leafy jungle plants and pools turned to sandy bogs.

In unison, the Pie Rats looked up at the thick canopy of trees in front of them.

'The glorious jungle,' Mr Tribble sighed. 'Walking should be much easier from here.' He stepped off a log onto a sandy patch of ground and immediately began to sink. 'H-h-help!' he cried, waving his paws in the air.

His ankles quickly disappeared.

'Quicksand!' Horace gasped. 'Stay perfectly still, Mr Tribble.'

Ignoring the advice, Mr Tribble thrashed his legs in a desperate attempt to escape. He sank to his waist.

Whisker lowered his body over the side of the log and stretched out his arm.

'Grab my paw,' he cried.

Mr Tribble made a frantic grab for Whisker, but his paw was well beyond reach. The hysterical mouse continued to panic and the quicksand rose to his chest.

'Stop moving or you'll go under!' the Captain shouted.

Mr Tribble kept moving.

'Mr Tribble! Stop!' Eaton squeaked.

With only his head and arms above the quicksand, Mr Tribble finally stopped.

'Don't move a muscle,' the Captain ordered. 'You'll only sink faster. Just relax your body and we'll get you out.'

Ruby removed a long candy cane from her backpack and passed it to Whisker.

'Essential survival item,' she said smugly. 'This should do the job.'

Whisker extended the sugary stick to Mr Tribble.

'Take hold of it,' he directed.

Mr Tribble grasped the candy cane in both paws.

'Pull me up!' Whisker cried.

Ruby and the Captain grabbed Whisker's legs, hauling him backwards and Mr Tribble's sandy body slowly rose from the quicksand.

'And I thought *students* had trouble following instructions …' Horace muttered, dragging Mr Tribble onto the log.

Mr Tribble straightened his glasses. 'Are you volunteering to be our new guide, Horace?'

'N-no,' Horace said, changing his tune. 'I'm quite happy in the middle of the pack.'

The Captain stood up and peered into the jungle. 'How far does the quicksand continue, Smudge?'

Smudge buzzed off into the undergrowth to explore. He returned several minutes later and landed on the rough bark of the log, repeatedly thrusting one arm towards the jungle.

'I think that means a long way,' the Captain said.

'Too far to leap,' Horace conceded, glancing down at his stumpy legs. '… though, we could use the bark to make a bridge.'

He tore off a large sheet of bark with his hook and held it up for the others to see.

'We'd require an enormous amount of bark to cross the quicksand,' Mr Tribble said, warily.

Ruby threw her paws in the air. 'Look around. Trees are everywhere!'

Whisker stared into the jungle and suddenly another idea came to him.

'Bridges don't have to be on the *ground*,' he said excitedly. 'There are endless branches, leaves and vines we can cross in the *air*.'

Mr Tribble wasn't convinced. 'We're not all trapeze artists with circus experience, Whisker.'

'Who needs experience?' Horace scoffed. 'If monkeys can swing off vines then so can rats and mice! It's either the trees or the quicksand.'

'Trees,' Mr Tribble replied quickly.

The Pie Rats formed a small bridge of bark over the quicksand and crossed to the nearest tree. Using strangler vines for paw holds they pulled themselves up the thick trunk. When they reached the upper branches they searched for hanging creepers.

'Here's the fun bit,' Horace said, grabbing a sturdy vine. 'Geronimo …!'

He leapt off the branch and swung through the air in a wide arc. In moments he had reached the next tree. Whisker was right behind him, surprised at how easy and enjoyable it was. With so many leaves and vines around him, even a small slip meant he had something to grab hold of.

'I could live up here!' Horace exclaimed, using his hook to catch a passing branch.

'It's still a long way down,' Mr Tribble gulped, holding on for dear life.

'Look!' Ruby exclaimed. 'Monkeys.'

Sure enough, to the left and right of the Pie Rats, small brown monkeys with white ear tufts and long banded tails appeared in the trees.

'Marmosets,' Mr Tribble pointed out. 'Good natured creatures, though a little cheeky at times.'

'Hello monkeys!' Horace shouted. 'We're swinging just like you!'

Whisker wasn't sure if the monkeys took offence to Horace's comment, but the next moment, several of them crashed into the rodents with angry hisses.

'Hey!' Horace exclaimed. 'Get your own vine. It's a free forest!'

Whisker ducked out of the way as a monkey in a rusty metal helmet tried to head-butt him out of the tree. His tail coiled around a vine, but before he had time to steady himself, he felt a hard kick to the head.

Losing his grip, he half jumped, half fell onto a branch and scrambled towards the safety of a huge tree. He'd nearly reached a hole in the trunk when the sound of bells filled his ears.

A monkey in a jester's hat plunged through the foliage, landing on Whisker with a *jingle, jingle, THUD!* Unable to support the weight of his attacker, Whisker's legs crumpled beneath him. He tried using his tail to shake the monkey off his back, but the side-to-side motions sent him sliding over the edge of the branch.

The monkey leapt clear as Whisker tumbled down, scratching helplessly at passing vegetation. As the ground raced towards him, he threw his paws forward to cushion the impact. Instead of the rough sting of quicksand, he felt the tightly woven strands of a net. It flexed under his weight, tightened, and then catapulted him into the air.

He somersaulted, twisted sideways and landed on his back. Dizzy and dazed, Whisker stared up at the treetops and thanked his lucky stars for safety nets.

Marvellous Marmosets

Whisker's safety was short-lived. Above him, the bodies of the Pie Rats dropped from the sky like meteors.

He rolled to his left as the Captain landed beside him, he rolled to his right as Mr Tribble and Eaton sprawled into the net. Finally, Ruby and Horace tumbled down together in a tangle of vines.

The net stopped bouncing.

'Rotten Pies to marmosets,' Horace groaned, untangling himself from Ruby. 'Life in the trees is so overrated.'

Smudge landed next to the Captain, waving his arms in frantic circles.

'It's time to depart,' the Captain said earnestly. 'Smudge says we're at the end of the quicksand.' The Captain clambered to his feet and promptly fell over again. The net was moving.

Whisker looked up. Long ropes stretched from the four corners of the net to the tops of the trees. Monkeys heaved on the ropes and the sides of the net moved upwards and inwards.

'Climb!' Ruby hissed, leaping up the side of the net.

Whisker clambered after her. The monkeys heaved harder.

Ruby was almost at the top when the four corners of the net closed in above her, blocking the forest light. In frustration, she kicked the net with her foot.

'Try your scissor swords,' Mr Tribble croaked from the gloom below.

Whisker reached for his sword. It wasn't there.

Ruby snarled, Horace gasped and the Captain groaned. Their scissor swords were gone! Despondently, Whisker and Ruby lowered themselves down.

'Take a look outside, Smudge,' the Captain whispered, 'and see what they're up to.'

Smudge squeezed through a small gap in the net. There was a *BUZZ* of wings, a dull *CLINK* and then silence.

'What was that?' Horace asked, confused.

'Judging by the echo, the lid of a pottery jar,' Mr Tribble guessed. 'At least it's not air tight.'

'There go our weapons *and* our spy,' Ruby muttered in annoyance.

'They haven't taken our matches,' Horace said, rifling through his backpack.

Ruby let out a long gasp of air. 'Don't even think about it, Horace! We need an escape plan, not a recipe for barbequed rat ...' She stopped. The net was lowering to the ground.

'Hold tight,' the Captain said. 'We may have a chance to negotiate our release. Monkeys are far friendlier enemies than cats.'

There was no other choice. The Pie Rats grasped the sides of the net as it collapsed on the forest floor. With a jerk, the net slid forward, scraping through the dirt and gathering momentum. It was soon bumping over logs, rustling through dry leaves and snaking around rocks. After what seemed like an eternity of battering and bruising, it finally came to a stop.

The dazed prisoners were dragged from their moving cell and tied against trees surrounding a small, grassy clearing. A tribe of marmosets stood in front of them, pointing and murmuring. Several metres from the prisoners, a small clay pot was placed on the ground and the Pie Rat's calico backpacks were piled nearby.

The monkey in the rusty helmet clapped his paws three times and the tribe of watching monkeys parted. Whisker heard the familiar jingle of bells as the monkey in the jester's hat skipped through the crowd, chanting, 'Manama badabba! Manama badabba!'

'What's he saying?' Horace whispered.

'Gibberish,' Mr Tribble muttered, 'It's not a language I'm familiar with.'

The jester continued, 'Koo-char koo-ching! Koo-char koo-ching!'

There was an excited roar from the crowd. The jester leapt to one side and four monkeys pranced towards the prisoners. The leader of the line wore a ridiculously large crown, sagging to one side. His shoulders were draped in a flowing purple cloak. The three monkeys following him wore royal headwear of lesser proportions.

'Manama yeee yuppa!' the jester cried.

The crowd gave an enthusiastic round of applause and the King in the oversized crown waved to the crowd before turning to face the prisoners.

'Great gallons of grape juice!' he exclaimed. 'Isn't this a splendid catch: Four rascally rats, two miniscule mice and a blowfly in a brown jar! We haven't had a haul like this since the echidna expedition of '88.'

'Wasn't that a wondrous time!' giggled a monkey in a gold tiara. 'All those spiny little critters scampering around while we stuffed them into the net!' She giggled again.

'I hated it, mother!' mumbled a monkey in a small crown. 'My paw got pricked and I couldn't peel a banana for three days ...'

'Poor prince party pooper!' teased a monkey in a silver tiara. 'You're the only heir in the world who needs a nurse to feed you fruit salad!'

'Shut it, sister!' he snapped. 'At least I'm not a pathetic little puppet. It's always *yes daddy dearest, no daddy dearest* with you.'

The monkey in the gold tiara nudged the King. 'Our children say such silly things when we have prisoners. Anyone would think they had to share a tree or line up to use the waterhole like common marmosets.'

'What, what?' the King muttered. Who's in the waterhole? Speak up, my dear Queen. I can't hear a thing.' He stuck his finger in his ear. 'Blasted tree sap! It's near impossible to get it out ... Wait a minute! I've just had a brainwave. Echidna spines! Brilliant! It's a revolution in ear cleaning. Sir Mecks, where are you?'

The monkey in the rusty helmet knelt before the King.

'Here, Majesty,' he said in a short, sharp voice.

'Sir Mecks,' the King said excitedly. 'You are to pluck every echidna spine from the prisoners and bring them to my royal tree at once!'

Sir Mecks glanced at the prisoners.

'Majesty,' he said. 'Prisoners – are – rodents.'

'Good gracious!' the King cried. 'You're absolutely, positively right. There's not an echidna in sight. I certainly won't be sticking rats' tails in my ears! Carry on with the punishment as planned.'

'Punishment?' Whisker gasped.

The King jumped.

'It-it speaks!' he gabbled, clutching his crown in both paws.

'Of course he can speak!' Horace fired back. 'We all can. And what's more important, we're all innocent!'

'Guilty,' Sir Mecks said in his metallic voice. 'Caught – trespassing.'

'Trespassing?' the Captain echoed. 'We didn't see any trespassing signs.'

'Great golden galoshes!' the King exclaimed. 'Of course you didn't see any signs. There weren't any. No one reads or writes in the Kingdom of Marvellous Marmosets!'

He turned to the crowd, raised his arms like a conductor and began to lead a chant:

Break all your pencils, tear up your maps.
Books are for grandmas who take morning naps.
Swing from a creeper, bask in the sun,
reading is banned in the kingdom of fun!'

There was a cheer from the crowd as the verse came to an end. Whisker shot a nervous glance at the pile of backpacks and whispered to Horace, 'We've got to get out of here before they get their map-tearing paws on *you-know-what.*'

'Don't worry,' Horace replied, without lowering his voice. 'That *clown* in the *crown* will forget we're even here before he finishes his next sentence.'

The King glanced sideways and straightened his crown.

'Clown?' he hissed. 'Don't you know who I am?'

Horace looked blank.

'Great grannies in ghettos!' the King gasped. 'I'm an international superstar. I'm King Marvownion, the third, exalted ruler of the Kingdom of Marvellous Marmosets.'

'All – kneel,' Sir Mecks droned.

'We can't kneel, you metal-headed mushroom!' Ruby snapped. 'We're tied to trees!'

The Queen broke into a fit of hysterical giggling.

King Marvownion shooed Sir Mecks into the crowd and resumed his introductions.

'Miserable maggots of the forest floor, I present to you the royal family: Queen Marmalade, Prince Marcabio and Princess Mayenya.'

The crowd cheered. The Queen gave the prisoners a royal wave with her paw and the children pulled ridiculous faces.

King Marvownion moved to the crowd. 'From our royal court, may I introduce Sir Mecks of the toadstool table and the unfathomable Jester Mimp.'

Mimp jiggled his bells and hopped on one foot singing, 'Mimp bimp tinkerty dink.'

Sir Mecks shut the metal visor on his helmet and did his best to ignore everyone.

The King proceeded to introduce the rest of the tribe: 'This is Mary, Mackie, Maggie, Maddie, Mandy, Mindy, Maisie, Manny, Marvin, Martin, Michael ...'

'That will do, my dear,' Queen Marmalade interrupted. 'You can't expect our prisoners to remember everyone's names. Why don't you skip to the execution bit?'

'What a splendid idea!' the King said, rubbing his paws together. 'What shall it be today? Hmm ... how about a ... beheading!'

Sir Mecks

Jester Mimp

Queen Marmalade

THE ROYAL COURT OF THE MARMOSETS

Prince Marcabio

Princess Mayenya

King Marvownion

'A BEHEADING!' gasped the Pie Rats.

'Boo!' chorused the crowd.

'Boring,' muttered the Prince.

The King's crown sagged further over his face.

'Don't take it personally, my dear,' the Queen said, gently patting his shoulder. 'We had a beheading last week. What about some variety? I'm partial to a hanging myself. It takes twice as long and the squirming is so entertaining.'

'A HANGING!' cheered the monkeys. 'We want a hanging!'

'FREEDOM!' pleaded the Pie Rats. 'Please let us go.'

The Prince and Princess both folded their arms and frowned.

'No one ever asks what I want,' Prince Marcabio complained.

'Me neither,' Princess Mayenya added.

'So what do you want?' Horace shouted over the noise, 'A royal pardon?'

'I want what *daddy dearest* wants,' the Princess replied, grinning angelically at her father.

'Brilliant,' Horace groaned. 'We're back to the beheading ...'

'Due-Esda!' Marcabio cried.

The cheering stopped. The entire tribe froze. Only Mimp's tiny bells rang through the silent forest. Whisker held his breath and stared expectantly at the Prince, hoping *Due-Esda* was Mimp's gibberish for *a swift release*.

'Great gardens of garlic!' the King exclaimed. 'What a smashingly stupendous idea!'

'Due-Esda!' cheered the ecstatic crowd. 'Due-Esda! Due-Esda!'

'Err, what *is* Due-Esda?' Whisker whispered to the Captain.

'I haven't the foggiest idea,' the Captain said, dumbfounded.

Ruby shrugged. 'Never heard of it.'

'It sounds sinister,' Horace moaned.

'Ask M-M-Mr Tribble?' Eaton stuttered.

The captives' eyes turned to Mr Tribble.

'Ooh my!' he gasped. 'I'm not sure you want to hear this, but Due-Esda is an ancient ball game played by two teams of five players. It uses a hard rubber ball and is commonly known by a different name ...'

Whisker's tail went icy cold. He knew the sport. He knew the name. They all did. It was the most brutal, barbaric and bloodthirsty ball game ever invented.

'Fellow prisoners,' Mr Tribble gulped, 'are you ready for a match of *Death Ball?*'

SIX

Death Ball

Death Ball, as its name suggests, involves *death* and a *ball*. In its modern form, the losing team receives a certificate of participation and a box of bandages. In its ancient form, losers were beheaded, burnt at the stake or exterminated using any method in vogue at the time.

'Pathetic prisoners!' the King cried excitedly. 'I hereby challenge you to a match of Due-Esda, the ancient game of death!'

'Death Ball! Death Ball! Death Ball to the death!' chanted the crowd.

The King continued, 'If you are victorious, you will be released into the wild jungle. If you are defeated, you will be hanged *and* beheaded!'

'A double execution!' roared the crowd. 'Our King is a genius!'

The Pie Rats looked at each other with a mixture of dread and bewilderment.

'We're in with a chance,' Horace said optimistically. 'Death Ball is a popular Pie Rat pastime, not a jungle sport.'

'I'm afraid you're mistaken, Horace,' Mr Tribble said

gravely. 'The rubber ball is made from latex sap from the *Castilla elastica* tree – a tree found in this very jungle. Historians believe that monkeys *invented* Death Ball. They've played it for centuries!'

Horace turned pale.

'Ah, excuse me, your royal hind leg,' he piped, trying to grab the King's attention, 'but what if we refuse your challenge?'

'What, what?' The King spluttered, sticking his finger in his ear. 'Did somebody say something? Goodness gracious! Speak up, whoever you are.'

Horace repeated himself in a loud voice. 'I SAID, WHAT IF WE REFUSE YOUR CHALLENGE?'

The crowd gasped. Queen Marmalade giggled awkwardly. 'What a silly little rat. No one refuses the King!'

King Marvownion strode over to Horace and pointed a sap-covered finger at him.

'Listen up, rude little rat. If you refuse my challenge, I'll skip the *ball* part of the game and jump straight to the *death*!'

'Th-that won't be necessary,' Horace squeaked. 'I-I was just checking ...'

'We accept your challenge,' the Captain said, before Horace could make things worse.

The crowd cheered and threw their paws in the air like their team had already won.

'Gobsmackingly good news!' the King said, licking his lips. 'Cut them down, Sir Mecks – but keep their pickpocketing paws tied behind their backs!'

The Pie Rats were roughly released from the trees and staggered into the centre of the clearing. The monkeys formed a tight circle around the perimeter to prevent them escaping. Long sticks were suspended between two trees at either end of the clearing to form goals and a hard rubber ball was brought forward and placed in a circle of dirt.

'So, who's played before?' the Captain whispered to his crew.

Horace and Ruby nodded. Mr Tribble and Eaton shook their heads.

'Death Ball is not an *approved* school sport,' Mr Tribble clarified.

'What about you, Whisker?' the Captain asked. 'Did the circus have an amateur team?'

'We, err … played a couple of times in the big top,' Whisker replied hesitantly. 'But it was touch, not tackle.'

'Touch Ball!' Horace exclaimed. 'That disgraceful game should be outlawed! You're playing in the big league now. It's rough and tumble with the big boys!'

'And girls!' Ruby snapped. 'Just because your precious sisters never played …'

'Ruby, please,' the Captain broke in. 'We're on the same team, remember? Save your aggression for the game – preferably for tackling the opposition.'

Ruby scowled. 'I hope that spoilt little Princess is playing. She won't stop staring at my eye patch!'

'That's the spirit,' the Captain smiled. 'A couple of good grapple tackles should rattle their game plan.'

Whisker felt ill. He'd escaped plenty of fights before, but it appeared he was stepping into the middle of a full-blown brawl. His tail began to tremble.

'First game jitters,' Horace whispered. 'We all get them. Don't worry, with a few matches under your belt, you'll be a pro. Death Ball is a Pirate Cup sport, so consider this game a training run for the big event.'

Whisker thought playing for his life *was* the big event.

'What about positions?' the Captain asked. 'We need a striker, a goal keeper, a centre, two wingers and a reserve. I believe our most dynamic player is Ruby. So I nominate her for centre.'

Ruby nodded. No one protested.

The Captain continued, 'On the wing, we require speed and agility, but not necessarily size. Horace and Eaton would be ideal candidates.'

Horace nodded his acceptance. Eaton rolled into a ball and let out a pained squeak.

'Eaton's not the sporty type,' Mr Tribble confessed. 'And neither am I, for that matter. Perhaps we could interchange as required?'

The Captain let out a long sigh. 'Very well. But we still need a striker and a goal keeper.'

'You're the best striker in the crew, Uncle,' Ruby pointed out, 'and seeing as Fred's not here, Whisker would make an effective keeper with his, err ... active tail.'

Whisker knew Ruby was paying him a compliment, so he responded with a half-smile.

'All agreed,' the Captain said. 'We have a team.'

'What about Smudge?' Horace gasped. 'We've totally forgotten about Smudge. He must still be in the pot.'

Horace rushed over to the pottery pot and tried to remove the lid with his toes. In the process, he knocked the vessel over and it shattered on the ground. Smudge clambered out of the rubble in a terrible rage and flew straight at Horace's shirt.

'Ouch! Aarh!' Horace cried. 'It hurts! It tickles! Stop it,

Smudge! It wasn't me. The monkeys did it.'

Smudge leapt out of Horace's shirt and zoomed towards the nearest monkey.

'Smudge! No!' the Captain bellowed. 'Come back here before you're squashed like a slug!'

Reluctantly, Smudge flew back to the Pie Rats and angrily perched on the rubber ball.

'Listen, Smudge,' Horace whispered. 'Are you strong enough to lift this ball?'

Smudge gripped the ball with six limbs and furiously beat his wings. The ball didn't budge. The buzz of wings grew louder as Smudge tried harder but the ball remained motionless. Monkeys began to point and laugh.

'Great gym-junkies!' the King exclaimed, stepping onto the field. 'What a ridiculous sight. Your filthy fly will never lift that ball. It's three times his puny size!'

'Smudge isn't puny,' Horace said, sticking up for him. 'He's extremely big for a fly. And it's not his fault your ball's above regulation weight!'

'Fiddlesticks!' the King cried. 'I made that ball myself.'

Smudge raised his tiny fists at the King and the King's eyes widened. 'Golly gosh! If your miniscule mascot wants a paw pounding that badly, he can join your team as a second reserve! He won't make an iota of difference to your piddly score line.'

'Untie us,' Horace demanded, 'and we'll find out.'

Sir Mecks untied the prisoners and the Pie Rats stretched their aching paws. Straightening his crown, King Marvownion proceeded to explain the rules.

'Cowardly captives, the rules of Due-Esda are as follows: One point is scored when the ball is kicked or hit under the crossbar between two trees. The ball may be carried,

80

thrown, kicked or passed from one side of the field to the other. It must *not* be hidden down one's trousers. I personally detest anyone wearing trousers, with of course the exception of baboons who have unsightly red bottoms...'

'Stick to the topic!' cried a voice from the crowd.

'What, what?' the King shot back. 'You're sick of the tropics? How rude! If you dislike the jungle that much, you can go and sit in an igloo. Your trouser-less bottom will look redder than a baboon's backside in less than a week, guaranteed!'

There was a dull murmur from the crowd and the King returned to the rules. 'A player possessing the ball may be tackled, tripped or wrestled until they release the ball. Players not involved in a tackle are limited to shoulder contact only. If the ball goes out of bounds, the crowd has the right to throw it to their favourite player ...'

'That won't be me,' Horace droned.

'Don't interrupt!' the King snapped. 'Where was I? Oh, yes. The ball is bounced in the centre circle at the beginning of each half and after each goal. Teams change directions at half-time.'

King Marvownion took a short stick and stuck it in the ground. Using his finger, he scratched four close lines from the base of the stick.

'This is a sundial,' he said proudly. 'I invented it. As the sun rotates around my marvellous kingdom, the shadow of the stick magically moves.'

Mr Tribble coughed awkwardly.

The King glared at him and carried on, 'When the shadow reaches the first line, the game begins. When it reaches the second line, we all stop for a cup of jungle tea.

When it reaches the third line, the second half excitement gets under way. And when it reaches the fourth line, the game is over and you all lose your heads! Any questions? No? Let the countdown begin!'

As the shadow of the stick crept towards the first line, the Pie Rats gathered in a huddle to discuss last-minute tactics. Whisker glanced over his shoulder to see the opposition walking onto the field. Predictably, the monkey's team consisted of the royal family plus Sir Mecks and Jester Mimp. A tribe member, whose name slipped Whisker's mind, acted as the referee and carried a short panpipe for his whistle.

'What's the game plan?' Horace whispered.

'We win,' Ruby said bluntly. 'And then we get out of this mad house.'

'Err, okay,' Horace said. 'Anything more specific?'

'Defence,' the Captain stated. 'We keep their goals to a minimum in the first twenty minutes while we discover their defensive weaknesses ...'

'We won't have twenty minutes!' Mr Tribble said frantically. 'Judging by the lines on the sundial, each half will be no longer than six or seven minutes!'

'Rotten pies to scurvy sundials!' Horace groaned.

'A short game's a survivor's game,' the Captain said calmly. 'Remember, defence is the key!'

As the panpipe blew for the start of the match, Whisker knew defence meant one thing: goalkeeping. He flexed his tail, loosened his limbs and prepared to defend to the death.

The ball bounced in the centre circle and Ruby leapt high into the air – Princess Mayenya leapt even higher. Gracefully, she plucked the ball from the sky and passed it to her brother on the wing.

Prince Marcabio caught the ball with one paw, using his free paw to defend against Horace. In a futile attempt to tackle the Prince, Horace threw himself, hook first, at Marcabio's legs. Deftly, Marcabio sidestepped to his left, leaving Horace clutching at blades of grass.

Tucking the ball securely under his arm, Prince Marcabio sprinted down the boundary line, sparking a Mexican wave from the crowd. Ruby tried to intercept him before he reached the forward pocket, but Princess Mayenya knocked her flying with a shoulder charge.

In the moment it took Ruby to recover, Marcabio paw-passed the ball to the King who bounce-passed the ball to the Queen via Mr Tribble's head. Mr Tribble somersaulted over the sideline and his glasses spun into the crowd. The crowd roared with laughter and threw him back into play without his glasses.

The frantic pace continued.

Prince Marcabio crossed infield to receive a long overhead pass from the Queen. He hastily tossed the ball into the air and prepared to slam it with his paw.

Scrambling off his wing, Horace made a desperate lunge for the Prince and ankle-tapped his left foot with his hook. Marcabio stumbled forward, missed the ball completely, and crashed to the ground. Seizing his opportunity, Whisker scooped up the ball while the Prince was still down.

'Over here!' Ruby shouted, breaking away from Mayenya on the right wing.

Whisker hurdled over Marcabio and kicked the ball as hard as he could in Ruby's direction. His foot stung as it made contact with the hard rubber but the impact sent the ball racing towards its target.

Ruby threw herself into the air, raising her paws to take the mark. But before she could secure the ball, Mayenya leapt over her head, pounding the ball into the crowd.

With an ecstatic chant of 'Mayenya! Mayenya!' the monkeys threw the ball back to the Princess. Revelling in the attention, she danced around Ruby, dummied to the King and then flick-passed the ball to Sir Mecks. Sir Mecks caught the ball in the centre of the field and charged, unmarked, towards Whisker's goal.

Turning defence into attack, Whisker sprinted infield to tackle the knight before he could strike. Sir Mecks attempted a rushed kick for goal but sent the ball hurtling into Whisker's chest.

Whisker tumbled backwards, clutching at the ball with his paws, and skidded across the grass. Startled, he looked up to see the Queen bearing down on him. With a powerful sweep of her leg, she kicked the ball straight out of his arms.

There was a triumphant roar from the crowd as the ball soared majestically through the goal posts.

Feeling like an oversized golf tee, Whisker thumped the ground in frustration.

'One-nil!' the referee cried.

'Substitute!' Mr Tribble squealed, staggering around blindly.

Eaton reluctantly came off the bench and took his place on the wing while Mr Tribble searched for his glasses in the crowd. Whisker brushed himself off and prepared for the next onslaught.

The panpipe whistled for the second bounce up. The monkeys won possession and went on the attack.

Desperately, the Pie Rats defended their line.

Whisker found it hard enough staying on his feet with all the barging and charging, let alone attempting to steal the ball. When the half-time whistle sounded minutes later, he wondered how they hadn't conceded a second goal.

'Great galaxies of gas!' the King exclaimed, as the teams walked from the field. 'Is it cup-of-tea time already? Gracious! I haven't knocked anyone unconscious yet!'

'Chin up, crew,' the Captain encouraged, removing a strand of monkey hair from his jungle tea. 'At least we've discovered their weakness.'

'What weakness?' Horace spluttered, spraying tea all over the Captain's jacket. 'They're unstoppable. We touched the ball three times in the entire first half and one of those was Mr Tribble's head!'

The Captain wiped the sticky liquid from his clothes and lowered his voice. 'I admit we need to work on our possession, but hear me out. The monkeys left their goal unattended the whole time we were on the field. One long-range kick is all we need to square things up.'

'*If* we ever get the ball,' Horace muttered.

SEVEN

Last Rat Standing

The teams assembled on the field for the second half with the ecstatic chants of 'Marmosets! Marmosets! No one beats a marmoset,' echoing through the clearing.

Queen Marmalade insisted she finish her cup of jungle tea at a leisurely pace, and was replaced by Jester Mimp on the wing. Smudge and Mr Tribble squirmed awkwardly beside her on the reserve bench.

The Pie Rats positioned themselves in a tight defensive structure within their own half. The monkeys prepared to attack and left their goal unguarded. The panpipe blew, the ball bounced, the crowd roared and the carnage began.

The Pie Rats did their best to repel the monkeys, tackling and tussling to the best of their ability. Even Eaton played like a desperate mouse with six-and-a-half minutes left to live. But as hard as they tried, they couldn't get that *one* clean kick away.

As the minutes wore down, the tension rose.

With a cheer from the crowd, Prince Marcabio caught the ball deep in the forward corner. He stepped around Horace, barged through Eaton and centred himself for a scoring shot.

Whisker dashed to his right to protect the goals. Out of nowhere, furry arms grabbed his legs. He struggled to free himself as his body rose into the air. Helplessly, he toppled face-first into a goal post, rebounding backwards into the path of the speeding ball.

WHACK! The ball hit Whisker square in the nose, ricocheting over the crossbar. Dazed and disoriented, he collapsed on the ground with the ring of bells in his ears.

'Sensational save!' Horace shouted.

'Illegal tackle!' Ruby hissed. 'Whisker didn't have the ball!'

'Yes he did!' roared the crowd. 'He was carrying it with his nose!'

A whistle rang out and the crowd lowered their voices to a dull murmur. Whisker looked up with watering eyes to see the referee standing over him. The referee pulled a yellow card from his armpit and bent down.

'Due-Esda is a sacred game,' he said in a stern voice. 'There are consequences for breaking rules. Yellow card offences attract a penalty shot at goal.'

Whisker felt his watering eyes turn to rivers of misery.

'I'm – I'm sorry,' he gasped, more to his teammates than to the referee.

'Sorry for what?' the referee grunted. 'Just tell me who tackled you and take your shot at goal.'

It took Whisker a few moments to register what he'd heard. It took him far less time to yell out Mimp's name and stagger to his feet.

The disgraced jester was booed from the field. The Queen tipped the rest of her tea over his head and, with a small hiccup, returned to the action. Sir Mecks took his position in the goal box and Whisker wasted no time in lining up his penalty shot.

'Give nothing away,' Ruby whispered in his ear. 'Pick a direction but look straight ahead.'

Whisker nodded and took three steps back.

Upper left corner, he told himself, staring at the centre of the goal.

The crowed went silent, awaiting the outcome. Whisker took his run up. Three steps and his foot made contact with a rubbery *THUD*.

The ball lifted off the ground, spinning to the left. Sir Mecks leapt high into the air. The nimble knight stretched out his paws to make the vital save but the ball brushed past his fingers, gliding through the upper left corner of the goal.

Whisker let out a sigh of relief. The crowd groaned.

'One-all,' the ref declared.

Horace gave Whisker a subtle hooks-up, but there was no post-goal celebration from the Pie Rats. One-all was hardly a winning score.

As Whisker made his way back for the bounce-up, he noticed the referee scratching a line in the dirt.

'I'm extending the sundial for extra-time,' the referee said with a sly grin, 'on the off chance we end in a draw ... it's in the rules!'

Whisker looked down in horror. The extra-time section was four times larger than the two halves. The Pie Rats would never survive. They would be annihilated on the field and then hung and beheaded and ...

Whisker felt his vision blur as his mind drifted into his memories. He needed a plan, and he needed it now ...

The crowd of monkeys vanished and a laughing circus

audience took their place. Two puppies stood in the centre of the ring, performing a comedic clown routine. Both puppies wore large baggy trousers. One had no belt. Whenever the first puppy tried to pull up his pants, the second puppy would tickle him until he dropped his trousers in a fit of hysterical laughter ...

Whisker's vision cleared. He looked at the bench. There were no playful puppies, only a tea-soaked jester, a beaten-up teacher and an irate blowfly.

'Substitute!' he cried. 'Last minute change.'

'What?' the Captain gasped. 'We can't use Mr Tribble. He's three-quarters concussed!'

'Not Mr Tribble,' Whisker said, 'Smudge!'

'But ...'

'There's no time, Captain. If I'm wrong, you can cut off my head and dangle me from a rope.'

'Very well,' the Captain muttered. 'But it's not just *your* head that's on the line.'

Eaton hurried from the field and Whisker whistled to Smudge. The excited blowfly entered the arena to the roar of laughter from the crowd, landing lightly on Whisker's shoulder.

'Listen, Smudge,' Whisker said in a low voice. 'The joke's on them. Remember what you did to Horace?'

Smudge punched his little fists together.

'Good,' Whisker said. 'Now I want you to do exactly the same thing to any monkey carrying the ball. But *only* if they're carrying the ball. Understand?'

Smudge didn't reply. He was already flying towards the centre bounce with a nasty gleam in his eye.

The panpipe shrilled and the game was on.

Princess Mayenya outjumped Ruby for the ball, but unlike the previous three bounces, Mayenya didn't get a quick pass away. Her feet had barely touched the ground when she started giggling uncontrollably and flapping her arms.

The ball slipped from her paws. Prince Marcabio picked it up and dashed from the centre circle. He tried to goose-step Horace, but broke out in a chorus of chuckles, dropping the ball.

Surprised at his good fortune, Horace pounced on the ball and looked for an unmarked player.

'This way!' the Captain shouted, scampering down the left wing.

Horace tried to hook-pass the ball but was sandwiched by the King and Queen. The ball popped free and bounced into the Queen's arms. She'd only taken a few steps when her usual giggles turned to howls of laughter.

'Oh my! Oh dear! It's wonderful! It's terrible! Stop tickling! No – keep going ...'

In hysterics, she threw her paws in the air and the ball soared over her head. The King made a hasty grab for it but tripped over Horace and landed on his crown.

With lightning speed, Ruby raced through the centre of the pack, taking the ball with her. She managed to raise her arm and slam the ball in the direction of the goal as Mayenya and Marcabio ploughed into her.

It wasn't a great shot and the ball skidded right, lurching towards the sideline. The Captain and Sir Mecks sprinted from opposite corners of the field, attempting to reach the ball first.

It was moving too fast for either of them and looked destined to bounce into the screaming crowd when, without warning, it hit something small and green in mid-flight.

The ball teetered in the air, spun to its left and shaved the inside of the goal post. Gobsmacked, the entire crowd stared in disbelief – Smudge had scored.

'Two-one,' the ref muttered with a disbelieving shake of his head.

The rats cheered. The royal family hissed. Smudge twitched uncontrollably on the ground.

'Medic!' Horace cried, rushing over to him.

Mr Tribble carried the stunned body of Smudge to the bench while the others looked on.

'He'll live,' the Captain said to his concerned crew. 'And so will we if we can hold them out for another thirty seconds.'

Whisker nodded and positioned himself in the goal box. Eaton replaced Smudge on the wing and Jester Mimp took Mayenya's place opposite Ruby, eager for a quick bounce-up. The entire marmoset team stood shoulder to shoulder behind him.

The referee raised the panpipe to his lips and blew. The ball bounced. Ruby jumped – Mimp waited.

With unopposed ease, Ruby plucked the ball from the air and landed delicately on her feet. With the power of a polar bear, Mimp crash-tackled her to the ground and the ball bounced free.

The monkeys took their cue and shoulder-charged the opposition. The Pie Rats tumbled over like they were nothing more than papier-mâché mannequins on a windy cliff top. Their trampled bodies were left sprawled across the field as the monkeys advanced. King Marvownion scooped up the ball and prepared to level the score. Only one rat stood in his way.

Whisker crouched in the centre of the goal square, his eyes fixed on the King.

Which way will you go? he thought.

The King held his line, moving into striking range. Whisker held his ground, waiting for a sign.

The ball dropped from the King's arm as he prepared to kick. His eyes flashed to the left and Whisker knew he had him.

Gotcha!

With expert precision, the King's foot made contact with the ball, launching it into the air. At the same moment, Whisker leapt to his left, raising his paws for the catch. As the ball rose higher towards the goal posts, Whisker realised he'd been cunningly out-played. The ball wasn't headed left, it was headed right.

In a final desperate effort to save the goal, he flicked his tail behind him, lassoing the ball. Like a cowboy restraining a stampeding bull, Whisker held on. He felt a stinging, tearing pain in his tail as it stretched to breaking point.

In agony, he crashed to the turf. The ball slipped from his grasp, bounced twice and stopped – only millimetres from the goal line.

With a *HISS* and a *HOWL*, the furious King made a desperate dash for the ball. Whisker mustered the last of his strength and pulled the ball towards him. He wrapped his arms and legs around the precious object and waited for the collision.

'*TOOT TOOT TOOOOT.*' A high pitched whistle filled the air.

Whisker lay still, listening to the sounds of running

footsteps. A body landed on top of him. Something hard dug into his back.

'We did it!' Horace cried, shaking Whisker with his hook. 'We knocked their royal socks off!'

Before Whisker could respond, he felt another hard thud as Ruby joined the pile.

'You're brilliant, Whisker!' she exclaimed. 'You *and* your deranged tail!'

For once, Whisker didn't blush. With his face squashed into the dirt, and two rats on top of him, all he could manage was a relieved sigh. One by one, the entire team threw themselves onto the winner's stack.

The crowd booed and hissed as the outcome of the match sunk in.

King Marvownion raised his arms to settle them.

'Marvellous monkeys of Marmosettia,' he shouted. 'Do not be dismayed ...'

'I don't like the sounds of this,' Horace muttered from the middle of the pile.

'Off with their heads!' chanted the crowd. 'Give us an execution!'

'Great ghouls in the gallows!' the King gasped. 'I can't execute them now, even if they are filthy rodents. There are rules to follow.'

'Who cares about the rules?' mumbled Mandy or Mindy or one of the others. 'You're the King!'

'What, what?' King Marvownion spluttered. 'Who's the King?'

Queen Marmalade giggled.

'Oh, yes,' he said. 'Golly gosh, that would be me. Right. Well, as the King, I can offer you something far more exciting than a dreary old execution ...'

'A rematch!' cheered the crowd. 'A rematch to the death!'

'Giant genies in jam jars!' the King exclaimed. 'Enough of the death talk! We're going to have a rip-roaring, nose-snorting victory celebration instead!'

'Victory!' cheered the crowd. 'Victory is ours!'

'Err, excuse me, King Marvellous Onion,' Horace squeaked, 'technically, it was *our* victory, not yours.'

'Don't be such a pretentious peacock,' the King growled. 'There's plenty of victory for everyone.'

'But ...' Horace began.

The Captain elbowed him in the ribs. 'Take as much victory as you want, Your Majesty. We're content with our ... bruises, aren't we, crew.'

'Oh yes,' cried the Pie Rats. '... extremely content! Lovely bruises ... best we've ever had!'

'Smashingly splendid!' the King declared. 'And seeing as you're all practically family now, I insist you stay for our little party. Bring out the jungle drums!'

With a *BOM BOM BOM* and a *BOMPER DEE BOM*, the drumming began. The royal family danced around the clearing in a conga line as the Pie Rats staggered to their feet.

'They're mad,' Horace muttered, twirling his hook around his ear. 'Totally, utterly bonkers!'

Golden Bananas

Mad monkeys were much easier to handle than *execution-crazed* monkeys. Whisker quickly forgot the whole death ordeal when the endless stream of exotic fruits and jungle delights rolled into the clearing. As his mother once told him, *Bruises feel better with a banana in your belly*!

Horace was soon dancing on a tree stump with Jester Mimp and Princess Mayenya, while Eaton and Mr Tribble played a game of *throw the banana peel over the sundial* with Prince Marcabio and Sir Mecks. King Marvownion and the Captain sat at a table and talked about Death Ball like they were best buddies from way back when.

'I hear that disastrously dangerous Pirate Cup is on again,' the King remarked, biting a banana without bothering to peel it. 'Are you entering?'

The Captain glanced at Ruby.

'We *do* have an opportunity to enter,' he said cautiously, 'but there are more pressing matters at hand ...'

'Grand goblets of goblins!' the King blurted out. 'Do you think they'd let *me* enter? I know I'm not *technically* a pirate, but golly gosh, I've strung up more innocent victims than the Sea Dogs and Penguin Pirates put together!'

Whisker had a strong feeling the King *wasn't* exaggerating.

'The entry fee for the Pirate Cup is enormous,' he said, trying to discourage the King from entering. 'I don't think they'd accept bananas.'

The King shrugged and stuffed the rest of the banana down his throat. The Queen lowered her piece of paw paw and giggled. 'Money's not a problem for us marmosets. We have oodles of treasure!'

'Really?' Ruby asked suspiciously.

'Great gulping gorillas!' the King spluttered. 'I just remembered. We have an entire trunk of treasure!'

'How big is this *trunk*?' Ruby asked in a matter-of-fact voice.

'It's a *tree* trunk!' the Queen laughed. 'You can have a look at it if you want. It's just over there.'

The King led Whisker, Ruby and the Captain past a garden of ferns and pointed to a huge hollow tree.

'Stick your snouts in there!' he chuckled. 'But if you touch a thing, I'll stuff your insides with chillies and feed you to an alligator!'

The rats put their paws in their pockets and peered inside. Whisker had never seen anything like it. He stared in awe at the glittering objects, his eyes wider than jewel-encrusted soup bowls. The entire tree was filled with treasure: diamonds, jewels, necklaces, bracelets and hundreds of golden bananas.

The King held one of the bananas.

'Solid gold!' he said, trying to bite it.

'Where did it all come from?' Whisker asked in amazement.

'Where?' the King exclaimed. 'From the snobs on the

hill, of course!'

'Snobs on the hill?' Whisker repeated.

'Those arrogant apes!' the King roared. 'Those conceited chimps! Those *I'm so fancy with my big brain* creatures that lived in the citadel!'

'The ancient kings?' Whisker gasped.

'*Former* kings,' the King corrected. 'I'm the only king left on this island!'

'Exactly *when* did you steal all this stuff?' Ruby enquired.

'Grubs in my gizzards!' he cried. '*I* didn't steal it. My ancestors stole it. No one's been up the hill for years. The place is a ramshackle ruin!'

'Just out of curiosity …' the Captain said in a casual voice. 'Are there any *keys* in your treasure trove?'

'What, what?' the King spluttered. 'Keys! Good grief no! What would I want with a key? I don't have any doors!' He threw the golden banana inside. 'Come along then. Let's have some *real* bananas. That one's given me a tooth ache!'

Reluctantly, Whisker pulled his eyes away from the sparkling fortune and followed the King back to the clearing.

The victory celebrations continued throughout the afternoon. Black clouds gathered overhead, prompting a raucous rain dance from the monkeys. As the night approached, the downpour arrived.

The exhausted Pie Rats sat yawning in the rain, while water pooled around them. Oblivious to their guests' discomfort, the monkeys continued their merriment.

Finally realising the Pie Rats had no desire to sleep in puddles, Queen Marmalade offered the visitors treetop hammocks for the night. The Pie Rats eagerly accepted and dragged their dripping bodies up the towering trees.

The hammocks hung in groups of three, protected from the rain by a roof of banana leaves. The Captain, Mr Tribble and Eaton took the lower group. Smudge curled up inside the Captain's backpack, and immediately fell fast asleep.

'Goodnight,' Whisker yawned, climbing past the Captain to the second group of hammocks. Horace overtook him and scrambled into the shelter first.

'I bags the trunk side!' he cried. 'At least if I sleepwalk I'll have the tree to protect me on my left and a sleeping body on my right!'

Ruby glared at Horace and snuggled into the hammock *furthest* away from the trunk. Whisker climbed into the middle hammock, looped his tail through the netting and hoped sleepwalking wasn't contagious.

It didn't take long for Horace to start muttering in his sleep. Whisker remained wide awake, listening to the pitter patter of raindrops above him and the sounds of drumming and chanting far below.

'Can't sleep either?' Ruby whispered.

'No,' Whisker replied softly. 'It must be the drumming.'

'Drums I can handle,' she said. 'It's that infuriating King and Queen I can't stand. Just listen to them.'

Whisker listened closely. Through the mumbles of Mimp and the chattering of Mackie, Maggie and the rest of the tribe, he heard the distinctive giggle of the Queen and the enthusiastic rants of the King.

'Great goslings in gumtrees!' the King shouted. 'We

should have another game of Death Ball tomorrow! Maybe the mudskippers would take up the challenge ...'

'Are all parents like that?' Ruby asked, rolling over to face Whisker. 'I never knew my mum and dad.'

Whisker shook his head. 'My parents aren't ...'

'What are they like?' Ruby asked casually.

Whisker wondered if Ruby was still dazed from the Death Ball match. She'd never asked about his family before.

'They're – normal,' he answered.

'No one's *normal*!' Ruby argued, before adding, 'I-I don't mean to imply your parents are crazy or anything.'

Whisker smiled. 'They're as normal as circus rats can be: no nooses in the top drawer, no guillotines in the closet –' He paused and tried to picture his parents. With the sound of rain in his ears, all he could see was their red boat disappearing into the cyclone.

'Your parents must be really clever,' Ruby said. 'You know, for you to have so many good ideas.'

'They're not smart like Mr Tribble or Pete,' Whisker admitted. 'They just know what to do with what they've got. My dad's good at inventing stuff. He makes all sorts of weird and wonderful inventions for the circus – like costumes with third arms that move on their own and hats that shoot confetti.'

Ruby's eye lit up. 'And what about your mother? Tell me about her ... I-I don't know much about mothers, only grumpy grandmas who get really cross when they find tiny specks of mud on skirts!'

'Sorry, *who* gets cross with mud on skirts?' Whisker asked, pretending he hadn't heard her.

'Fair call,' Ruby said. 'Like grandmother, like

granddaughter ...' She sighed. 'My gran's ok, she's just short-tempered and impatient.'

'Another family trait?' Whisker said playfully.

'I thought we were talking about *your* family!' Ruby snapped.

'Ok, ok,' Whisker said, not wanting to be hurled out of his hammock. 'My mother, Faye, was a fruit and vegetable grower. She knows lots about weather and nature and healthy eating ...'

'Is that why you chose the vegetable sails?' Ruby cut in.

Whisker grinned. 'My mother always said that *vegetables would keep me alive!*'

Ruby rolled her eye. 'Save the bad jokes for Horace ... But tell me, how did a green paw like your mother meet a circus rat like your father?'

'Well,' Whisker began, 'when the circus came to Faye's village in Freeforia she set up a roadside stall not far from the big top. My father, Robert, who was supposed to be mending tents and costumes, bought vegetables from her every morning and every evening, even if she only had mouldy potatoes left!'

'He clearly *wasn't* there for the potatoes!' Ruby laughed.

'Try telling Mum that,' Whisker said. 'She's a bit naïve when it comes to that sort of thing. Anyway, there's no currency in Freeforia, so Robert traded his inventions for Faye's fruit and vegetables. At the end of two weeks he was running out of wind-up potato peelers and temperature-controlled flowerpots to give her.'

'Why didn't he just tell her how he felt?' Ruby asked. 'It's much easier than pretending he liked rotten potatoes!'

'Good point,' Whisker agreed, 'but Dad's pretty clueless in that department, too.'

Ruby rolled her eye again. 'So what happened?'

'Being a poor farmer's daughter,' Whisker explained, 'Faye had never been to the circus before, so Robert promised her the best seats in the house for the final show.'

'Like a date?' Ruby said.

'I guess,' Whisker shrugged. 'When the night finally arrived, Robert smuggled Faye through the back door of the big top and the two of them watched the performance from the rafters.'

There was a rumble of drums below. Whisker glanced down at the festivities.

'It's a bit like us in this tree,' he said innocently. 'We've got the best two hammocks in the house!'

'Except there are *three* of us,' Ruby pointed out.

'OH!' Whisker gasped, realising what he'd just implied. 'Yes, of course, Horace ... three *friends* in a tree.'

'Goodnight, Whisker,' Ruby yawned, closing her eye. 'Thanks for the bedtime story ...'

'Night,' Whisker squeaked, with redder cheeks than a baboon's bottom.

He lay awake for some time, staring at a banana leaf and wishing he'd inherited a smooth-talking tongue from his parents.

Rays of morning sunlight poked through gaps in the jungle canopy. Water dripped from leaves into puddles far below. The occasional snore echoed through the still forest.

Whisker uncoiled his tail from his hammock and sat up. Horace opened his eyes, yawned, closed his eyes again and pretended he was still asleep. Ruby was nowhere in sight.

Fastening his backpack, Whisker climbed down from the tree. He quietly pushed through the ferns on the forest floor and discovered Ruby next to a large rock, cleaning a pile of scissor swords.

'I found our weapons in a hollow log,' she said, raising her eye. 'They'll rust in no time in this weather. *Scissor swords must be sharp at all times*, remember?'

She handed Whisker his green sword and lowered her voice. 'I don't trust that royal family one bit. If they try any monkey business today, we'll be ready.'

Whisker nodded. There was a rustle of ferns behind him. Ruby grabbed the nearest sword and pointed it at the plants.

'Who's there!' she hissed.

'Only a dog looking for his bone,' Horace yawned, stumbling out.

Ruby flashed Horace a look of irritation and threw him his blue-handled scissor sword. He clumsily caught it with his hook.

'Don't drop it in the mud!' she snapped. 'I've been up since before dawn polishing it for you.'

'Alright, alright, I'll keep it clean,' he mumbled, sticking it in his belt. 'Now who's up for breakfast?'

'Breakfast will have to wait,' whispered a deep voice from behind the rock.

The three rats turned to see the Captain stepping out of the undergrowth.

'Smudge has discovered a path to Silver Falls,' he

explained. 'An early start would be advantageous.'

'An early start or a *quick getaway*?' Horace muttered.

'I'd leave a note,' the Captain said, unimpressed, 'but who would read it? Jester Mimp?'

'Point taken,' Horace conceded.

'Mr Tribble and Eaton are already on the path,' the Captain said earnestly, 'so we'd best hurry.' He picked up his black scissor sword and disappeared into the bushes with Ruby and Whisker on his heels.

'It's lucky I had a big dinner,' Horace sighed, staggering after them.

The track was overgrown with large-leafed plants and matted vines. It was clear the monkeys preferred travelling through the tree tops than overland. Although the plants obscured their view, the rats had no doubt about the direction they were hiking. The unmistakable roar of the waterfall could be heard half a jungle away.

The rats caught up with the mice as they neared Silver Falls. The jungle opened out onto a wide riverbank. Lush patches of grass grew to the edge of a fast-flowing river where water swirled over submerged rocks to form frothing rapids.

Towering over the river stood a mighty cliff. Crumbling boulders and mossy plants covered its weathered face. A torrent of water cascaded from its hazy heights, thundering to the rocks below. From a pool at the base of the cliff, a fine spray rose into the air, shimmering in the morning sunlight. Silver Falls was at once both glorious and terrifying. The Pie Rats had two options: cross the river, or climb the falls.

'I say we climb,' Horace declared, pointing to the cliff with his hook. 'Raging rapids and short-statured rats make a lethal combination.'

Mr Tribble agreed. 'There's plenty of vegetation to grab hold of on the cliff face, and we can cross the river upstream where the water is calmer.'

No one needed any further convincing. They tightened their backpacks and crept to the base of the cliff. At close range, the roar of the water was almost deafening.

'KEEP AWAY FROM THE WATERFALL,' the Captain bellowed. 'ONE SLIP AND YOU'RE HISTORY!'

The Pie Rats edged further away from the spray-covered rocks, heading for the drier sections of the cliff. Small tufts of grass growing between boulders provided paw-holds, but the dirt was loose and the grass fell away like moulting fur in springtime.

As the Pie Rats climbed higher, a wide overhanging rock forced them closer to the waterfall. Trickles of water seeped from cracks and dribbled over slippery, moss-covered stones, making every move even more treacherous.

With their eyes fixed on the cliff, none of the climbers noticed the sky darkening or the storm clouds rolling in. They were only halfway up when the heavens opened and the rain pelted down. It was impossible to continue.

'FIND A DRY SPOT!' the Captain cried.

Whisker looked around. There wasn't a dry spot. The rain blew in from over his shoulder, saturating the entire cliff face. He heard a loud scraping sound and turned to see Horace sliding from a rock, frantically scratching for holds.

Whisker threw out a paw and grabbed the tip of Horace's hook, jerking him to a halt. Dangling in midair, Horace kicked his stumpy legs in an attempt to find a foot hold. Whisker felt himself slipping.

'HOLD STILL!' he shouted, trying to regain his balance.

Horace stopped squirming but gravity took hold. With the weight of Horace pulling him down, Whisker's upper body began toppling towards the falls.

He opened his mouth to scream, but the Captain's strong arms grabbed his shoulders, dragging him back. Ruby helped Horace onto a stable rock and the soggy party clung on for dear life as the rain grew heavier.

'HEAD FOR THE FALLS!' Mr Tribble cried.

'WHAT?' the Captain spluttered.

'UNDER THE OVERHANG,' Mr Tribble yelled back. 'IT'S THE SAFEST PLACE!'

Whisker squinted through the driving rain. Mr Tribble was right. The overhanging rock extended into the waterfall. The water gushed *over* the rock, but *under* it was a small cavity. It was wet and slippery, but protected from the pelting rain by the wall of water.

The Pie Rats shuffled closer. Whisker watched, perplexed, as one by one his companions squeezed into the tight cavity and vanished from sight.

NINE

Silver Thieves

At first, Whisker had a horrible feeling his companions had been washed into the waterfall. But as he crawled into the cavity, he saw exactly where they had gone. Hidden from sight by the stream of water, was the entrance to an enormous cave.

Whisker scurried into the gloom, gasping in awe at the wide cavern in front of him. In the flickering light of Eaton's lantern, the full glory of the subterranean chamber was revealed.

Stalactites of every shape and size hung from the high ceiling. Some took on the appearance of delicate sewing needles, while others resembled battle-weary broadswords. Groups of stalactites hung together like upside-down beds of nails. Rising from the floor were stalagmites of equal grandeur – hard, wet rock, growing ever upwards as the stalactites dripped mineral-rich water upon them.

Where the stalagmites and stalactites had joined, great columns extended from the floor to the ceiling. They rose like majestic marble pillars, each decorated with an intricate stone façade. The lantern light sparkled off a thousand rippled surfaces and the Pie Rats stared in amazement.

Eaton directed his lantern to the far corner of the cave where a dark passage extended into the darkness. Strange round objects covered the floor. Some were encrusted in the hardened rock of stalagmites, others lay in shallow pools. All of them were silver.

'Ratbeard's reward!' the Captain exclaimed. 'We've just discovered the silverware of Silver Falls!'

The Pie Rats rushed over to examine the booty. There were plates and platers, saucers and bowls and a vast collection of ornate serving dishes.

'They've been here forever,' Horace said, trying to dislodge a platter from a stalagmite.

Whisker pulled a plate from a puddle and shook off the water.

'Solid silver?' he pondered. 'What's it doing here?'

'It looks like a thieves' lair,' Mr Tribble said, wiping mud off a bowl. 'I suspect the marmosets used it to hide the treasure they stole from the citadel.'

'Not recently,' Horace panted, still struggling with the platter.

The Captain pointed to the passage. 'If the cave is a hiding spot between the citadel and the lower jungle, then perhaps there is another entrance, one easier to access from the mountain.'

'There's no harm in looking,' Horace said, giving up on the platter. 'I'm happy to crawl around in the darkness if it saves me climbing that death-trap of a cliff again!'

'What about the treasure?' Ruby asked. 'It would be a travesty to leave it all here, especially with the Pirate Cup just around the corner.'

'And there's certain to be important historical artefacts among the items,' Mr Tribble added.

The Captain thought for a moment.

'It's not every day we stumble into a silver treasure-trove,' he admitted. 'And considering we're flat broke, I see no harm in taking a few *unclaimed* trinkets with us.'

Hurriedly, the Pie Rats stuffed their backpacks full with silverware. Plates and saucers proved the easiest things to pack. Horace found a pile of knives and forks under a serving bowl and managed to squeeze in an entire dinner set.

'Pies always taste better with silver service …' he mused, proceeding into the passage.

While the others filed after Horace, Whisker lingered in the cave, staring longingly at four silver side plates he'd scrounged from a puddle. Their dull, tarnished surfaces reminded him of the humble tin plates he'd eaten off as a child. He ran his finger over an engraved edge. Happy memories of dinnertime conversations filled his mind.

'Four plates,' he said to himself, finally stowing the items. 'One for each member of my family.' With a yearning sigh, he fastened his bag and crept into the darkness.

The tunnel moved steadily upwards, opening out into a small cave before resuming its twisting path towards the surface. The roof of the passage lowered and the Pie Rats found themselves crawling on their paws and knees through puddles of mud. Their bulging backpacks scraped on low rocks, forcing them onto their stomachs.

'What is it with this island and mud?' Ruby complained, sliding out of a sloppy brown bog.

'Well …' Horace began.

'Light ahead!' Eaton exclaimed.

Sure enough, a speck of light glowed ahead of them. As they slithered forward, it grew larger and brighter.

The Pie Rats' eyes stung as they tumbled into the misty sunlight. The dull murmur of the waterfall echoed from far below. They were high up on the mountainside, on the opposite side of the river. Mountain plants lay all around them and the entrance to the passage was no more than a fern-covered crack between two large rocks. Whisker wondered if they could even find it again.

'The rain has finally cleared,' Horace yawned, stretching his mud-covered arms above his head.

'For now,' Mr Tribble said cautiously. 'But we won't know if it's coming or going with all this mist around.'

'Is there a direction we can take?' the Captain asked. 'I can't see my paws in front of my face.'

Mr Tribble took out a compass.

'The main track to the citadel cuts inland to avoid the falls,' he said. 'It should be due west of here.'

'West it is,' the Captain said decisively. 'Scissor swords at the ready. We're going cross-country!'

The Pie Rats hacked and slashed their way through the dense jungle undergrowth. Ruby led the way with Smudge flying blindly above her.

'Stupid mud,' she grunted, flicking ferns out of the way. 'Stupid mist!'

'Stupid *tour guide*,' Horace muttered, copping a fern in the face.

They reached a spot where the mist wasn't so thick. Eaton suddenly stopped in his tracks and sniffed the air.

'What is it?' the Captain whispered, staring into the wispy haze.

'E-e-eyes,' Eaton gasped. 'D-d-dozens of eyes …W-w-watching us.'

The Pie Rats froze.

'Stay together,' the Captain hissed, raising his sword. 'Strike first, think later, understood?'

The crew understood and huddled together in the mist, swords ready, awaiting the ambush. Nothing stirred. Whisker began to wonder what was out there. *Marmosets? Two-toed sloths? Or something worse? Did they have weapons ... or poison darts?*

'Look,' Horace whispered.

The mist slowly parted and the trees grew clearer. Staring down at them were huge black eyeballs.

'D-d-drop bears!' Horace choked. 'We're d-d-done for!'

Whisker felt his tail coil around his leg. Fearlessly, Ruby took a step towards the trees.

'No, Ruby!' the Captain pleaded.

Ruby stopped as the mist closed in. She turned to face Horace and gave him a horrified look. Horace's eyes widened.

'You s-s-saw them, too?' he trembled.

Ruby moved closer and slowly opened her mouth.

'BOO!' she cried.

Horace jumped a full tail's length into the air. Eaton jumped a tail and a half. Ruby dropped both swords on the ground and roared with laughter. 'Oh, Horace! Oh, Eaton! If only you could see yourselves. It's the funniest thing I've ...'

'RUBY!' the Captain thundered. 'What the Tasmanian devil is wrong with you?'

Ruby kept laughing. '... nothing's wrong with me, Uncle ...'

'What about those – those creatures,' the Captain gasped.

'Creatures!' Ruby howled in hysterics. 'Gigantic, huge, enormous *creatures* –' She paused to catch her breath.

Eaton huddled under Mr Tribble, utterly terrified. Horace hid behind his hook and Smudge crawled under a leaf. Whisker, however, stood his ground and shook his head at Ruby.

'Oh, come on, Whisker!' she cried. 'It's hilarious!'

'What's she gabbling on about, Whisker?' the Captain asked in confusion.

Ruby gave Whisker a look that said, 'Don't tell!'

Whisker knew exactly what Ruby was talking about and thought it was best if he put the others out of their misery.

'We're perfectly safe, Captain,' he said slowly.

The Pie Rats cautiously raised their heads to see the mist rolling back and the trees coming into view. There were no drop bears, two-toed sloths or murderous monkeys in sight – but there was something *watching* them. Bunches of bright red fruit hung from the trees. Some of the fruit was open, revealing large black seeds with white coverings. They looked exactly like eyeballs.

'Pete's missing herb,' the Captain groaned. 'I should have known.'

'But what happened to the drop bears?' Horace squeaked.

'Drop bears don't exist,' Ruby laughed, 'but gullible rats do!'

'I think we've had enough of your little joke, Ruby,' the Captain said sternly. 'And seeing as you and Whisker are both *eyeball* experts, you can collect half a bag of shelled seeds for Pete.'

Ruby stopped laughing. 'I'd *love* to help, Uncle, but the backpacks are filled to the brim with silverware. We couldn't possibly fit a single seed in!'

The Captain removed his backpack and placed it on the ground.

'My backpack has plenty of room for seeds,' he said.

'No, it hasn't,' Ruby insisted.

The Captain opened his bag and removed a large apricot pie.

'Now it has,' he said with a wide grin. 'I'm starving!'

While the Captain and his fellow prank victims sat down for an early lunch, Ruby and Whisker disappeared into the mist to collect eyeballs.

'Say hello to the drop bears for me!' Horace cried out. 'I'll save a piece of pie for you – *Whisker.*'

'Stupid drop-bears,' Ruby muttered, slicing the tops off small plants. 'Stupid eyeballs.'

'Leave the bad jokes to Horace, next time,' Whisker advised. 'Your advice, not mine.'

Ruby turned around and glared at him.

'Horace *is* the bad joke!' she huffed.

Whisker decided to drop the subject and scrambled up the nearest eyeball tree. He knew the sooner he collected the seeds, the sooner he'd get his slice of pie.

Collecting seeds was easier said than done. Once Whisker reached the top of a tree, he had to search every branch for ripe fruit (of which there were very few), and throw them down to Ruby for shelling. The Captain's backpack filled at a remarkably slow pace.

'How are we looking?' Whisker asked, climbing down the eleventh tree.

Ruby gave him a sour look. 'Half empty. We need a decent tree of eyeballs to fill up the bag.'

'I may have spotted one from the air,' Whisker said, wishfully. 'It's on the eastern side of a gully not far from here.'

'Lead the way,' Ruby said, hoisting the bag over her shoulder.

The two rats trekked in the direction of the gully and the ground steadily dropped away. The gully plants grew thick and lush and it was hard for the rats to see where they were headed.

'Down here,' Whisker said, descending the slope. He pointed through the leaves to a huge bunch of ripe fruit. 'There it is!'

Ruby dropped the bag and took off her swords.

'I'll lend you a paw,' she said eagerly. 'There are plenty of eyeballs for both of us.'

Whisker removed his sword and scaled a nearby vine. Its leaves were long and springy and anything but stable. He cautiously checked his footholds before proceeding upwards. Ruby, eager to reach the fruit, leapt from leaf to leaf like they were small trampolines.

Whisker reached the highest leaf of the vine. Balancing on one foot, he stretched out for the trunk of the tree. Before he could grab it, Ruby bounced onto the leaf. The leaf dipped under their weight and Whisker tumbled backwards into Ruby. The two rats slid over the side of the leaf, crashed through the foliage and plunged headfirst into a pool of sticky liquid.

TEN

Rat-eating Plants

Gasping for air, Whisker burst from the surface of the pool and pulled Ruby's head out.

'Eeeyeew!' she coughed, spitting out a mouthful of the strange liquid. 'W-what is this stuff?'

Whisker tried to steady himself. His toes barely reached the bottom of the pool. The ground beneath him felt soft and rubbery.

He looked around, puzzled. The pool had high purple walls extending to a round opening above. A large leaf-like shape hung over the pool, concealing it from the air.

'It's not water, whatever is it,' Whisker said, swishing his tail through the substance.

'I think it's some kind of acid,' Ruby guessed, trying to scale the slippery wall.

With no pawholds, she lost her grip and splashed back into the pool. The liquid shook, the walls vibrated.

'It's moving!' she gasped.

'Only if we move,' Whisker said, beginning to understand. 'Ruby, I think this is the rat-eating plant they warned us about.'

'Eeeyeeew!' Ruby cried again. 'We must be in its *stomach*, which means all of this liquid is …'

'Digestive juices,' Whisker said grimly. 'Slowly dissolving our bodies.'

'We've got to get out!' Ruby gasped. 'Quick, give me your sword.'

'I-I don't have it,' Whisker confessed. 'I left it next to the bag.'

'Why would you do a thing like that?' Ruby snapped. 'Don't you know it's dangerous out here?'

Whisker was taken aback. 'Hey, you can't talk! You removed your swords first.'

'That's different,' Ruby huffed. 'Besides, you should know better than to follow my lead. You're supposed to be the sensible one in the relationship!'

'Relationship?' Whisker gasped. 'I didn't know ...'

'JUST COME UP WITH A PLAN TO GET US OUT OF HERE!' Ruby bellowed.

'Okay, okay,' Whisker mumbled. 'You don't need to shout. Just climb on my shoulders and see if you can reach the top.'

Ruby frowned. 'That's it? Your brilliant escape plan?'

'Yes,' Whisker said bluntly. 'Not all great plans involve fancy props and explosions ... but if you'd prefer something more exciting we can wait until our bodies dissolve and escape through the veins of the plant ...'

'Give me a paw up, will you,' Ruby snapped.

Whisker helped Ruby onto his shoulders. The skin on his paws and feet stung in the acidic liquid. He hoped he had time to escape in one *solid* piece.

'I can't quite reach the top,' Ruby said in frustration.

'Try leaping off my shoulders,' Whisker suggested. 'I'll crouch down and give you a boost.'

'If you insist,' Ruby said, unconvinced. 'Squeeze my foot

when you're ready.'

Whisker took a deep breath, closed his eyes and submerged under the liquid. He waited for the ripples to settle and, with a quick squeeze of Ruby's foot, launched himself upwards. As his head pierced the surface he felt Ruby leap from his shoulders.

He half expected her body to crash down on top of him, but when he looked up he saw Ruby hauling herself over the rim of the plant.

'Have fun dissolving!' she laughed, disappearing from sight.

Whisker stood in the middle of the pool, slowly dissolving. There was a noise from above and a strand of vine splashed into the liquid.

'Climb!' called a voice.

Whisker climbed like he'd never climbed before. In moments, he'd scrambled over the rim of the purple prison, scooted down the vine and was throwing himself into the nearest rainwater puddle.

Ruby splashed down next to him.

'Digestive juices are wonderful for removing mud,' she remarked, rinsing herself off.

'And skin!' Whisker added, staring at his red feet.

Ruby shrugged. 'Oh well. What doesn't kill you makes you *cleaner!*'

'I thought we banned the Horace jokes?' Whisker groaned. 'Now, if you'll excuse me, I've got eyeballs to collect – *alone.*'

Two extremely clean and rather hungry rats arrived back at the picnic site.

'No drop bears then?' Horace said from his spot in the sun. 'We saved you some pie but it was hard to keep the fly away.'

Smudge shook his tiny arms at Horace as if to say, *your piece of pie was seventeen times the size of mine!*

'You were gone a while,' the Captain said, eying them suspiciously. 'You weren't planning another practical joke, were you?'

'We had *stomach* troubles,' Ruby blurted out. '*Nasty* stomach troubles.'

'That's terrible!' Horace cried, leaping to his feet. 'I guess you'll pass on the pie then?'

Ruby moved her paw to the handle of her sword.

'O-on the other hand,' Horace gabbled, 'pie is very good for stomach troubles …'

Eagerly, Ruby sat down to eat her pie. Whisker sat next to her, fidgeting awkwardly. His tail felt as tender as his toes. Mr Tribble stared at him and held up a page from his notebook.

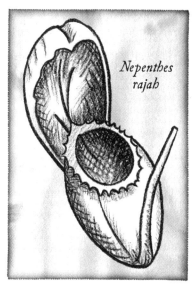

Nepenthes rajah

'I take it you ran into one of these?' he said, pointing to a sketch of the rat-eating plant.

'*Fell* into one,' Whisker clarified. 'Do you know what it is?'

'It's called a *Nepenthes rajah*,' Mr Tribble explained. 'It's an insectivorous pitcher plant. You're lucky you're a mammal and not an insect. Flies digest much quicker …'

Whisker felt relieved. Smudge looked terrified.

'When did you draw the picture?' Ruby asked.

'Just now,' Mr Tribble replied. 'Eaton and I saw several specimens while we were collecting herbs.' He held up a bundle of roots. 'I'm not one for lying in the sun, so I decided to hunt for Pete's second herb. Digging up roots is far easier than scrambling up trees or escaping from pitcher plants!'

'I still prefer sun baking …' Horace yawned.

Ruby flashed Horace an unimpressed look and recited, '*A lazy Pie Rat is a dead Pie Rat, the Pie Rat code.*'

Horace got the hint and clambered to his feet.

The Pie Rats continued on their jungle trek with the usual mumbles, grumbles and rude remarks they had all come to expect. Mr Tribble's prediction was accurate and the companions soon reached the main track. It was extremely overgrown. The only things that distinguished the ancient path from the rest of the undergrowth were the carved steps leading up the mountainside.

Horace, who'd clearly run out of conversation topics, decided to count every step: 'One, two, three, four …' Time passed slowly. '… one thousand two hundred and sixty two, one thousand two hundred and sixty three, one thousand two hundred and … oh! That's the last step.'

'What a shame!' Ruby said sarcastically. 'I was *so* enjoying your soothing voice.'

'I could count footsteps?' Horace suggested.

'And I could hurl you over the ravine,' Ruby said, deadpan.

Horace let his feet do the talking.

'Speaking of the ravine,' Mr Tribble said, holding up his compass, 'the bridge should be straight through those bushes.'

Hurriedly drawing both swords, Ruby slashed through the undergrowth to reveal a rocky plateau leading to the edge of a deep chasm. On the opposite side of the ravine, a cliff of crumbling rock ran up the side of the green mountain like a deep, fleshy scar. A dilapidated suspension bridge spanned the huge gap.

'Come and take a look, Horace,' Ruby cried, scampering to the edge of the ravine. 'If you lean over far enough, you can see the river below. It's such a *long* way down. One little slip and you're ...'

Horace pressed himself against the bushes and squeaked, 'I'll-I'll be fine on my own over here, away from danger ... and dangerous crewmates.'

'Suit yourself,' Ruby shrugged, moving over to the swing bridge. She gave a weathered plank a firm tap with her foot. 'It feels solid enough.'

'I've seen better,' the Captain remarked, joining her on the edge. 'The ropes are frayed, half the planks are missing, and I doubt anyone's crossed it in years.'

Mr Tribble peered through his dirty glasses.

'Hmm. The planks *are* a concern,' he admitted, 'especially in the centre of the bridge. But the four main ropes appear quite sturdy ... It's definitely worth a try.'

'Look at you!' the Captain laughed. 'Emmie would be so proud. The timid teacher turned brave adventurer!'

'I'm *not* volunteering to go first, if that's what you're implying,' Mr Tribble said firmly.

The Captain looked down at Eaton.

'You're a light little fellow, Eaton,' he said casually.

Eaton shook his head furiously.

'I'll go,' Horace whimpered, untangling himself from

the bushes. 'I'm small and expendable and destined to die – loveless and alone.'

'Oh, stop your moping!' Ruby scolded. 'No one thinks you're expendable. And I'm sure there's one girl out there who appreciates your *unique* sense of humour.'

'You really think so?' Horace said, perking up.

'… yes,' Ruby muttered through clenched teeth. 'But she's not *me*, so don't get any funny ideas!'

'I wouldn't dream of it,' Horace replied, giving Whisker a subtle wink.

'Good!' the Captain said gruffly. 'You've got more important things to do – like getting on that bridge!'

Horace removed his backpack and approached the bridge.

'It *is* a long way down,' he said, peering over the ravine.

'Stick to the sides,' Mr Tribble advised. 'And keep a paw on the handrail at all times.'

'Or a hook,' Horace said, looping his hook around the thick rope. 'Wish me luck!'

He stepped forward. Wooden planks creaked under his weight as he tiptoed across the bridge. Gentle vibrations pulsed through the ropes, sending loose planks plummeting to the river below.

'I'm okay!' he exclaimed with every falling plank.

The crossing seemed to take forever, but after a few tense minutes, Horace reached the opposite side of the ravine.

'NOTHING TO IT … *TO IT … TO IT …*' his voice echoed back.

'Splendid,' the Captain said. 'So who's next – with a backpack this time?'

The mice looked hesitant and Ruby appeared to be in two minds about the whole thing.

'I'll go,' Whisker volunteered. 'It's no worse than the

120

high ropes at the circus.'

'Follow Horace's exact path,' Mr Tribble stressed.

'And remember to use your tail,' Ruby added. 'It always gets you out of trouble.'

'When it's not getting me *into* trouble,' Whisker said under his breath. 'I'll see you on the other side.'

Whisker stepped, ever so lightly, onto the bridge. The small figure of Horace waved enthusiastically down to him and Whisker realised just how high Horace was. The far side of the ravine followed the slope of the mountain and the bridge rose up and up and up.

Every step led Whisker further from the safety of the cliff and closer to the danger zone in the centre of the bridge. He stuck to the right side of the planks, gripping the handrail with his paw. His tail slid over the rope behind him, stabilising his movements.

The gully wind arrived with a howling gust as Whisker reached four missing planks in the middle of the bridge. He carefully stepped onto the footrope and shimmied along. His upper body swayed back and forth under the weight of the backpack, but the handrail kept him from falling.

He reached a solid plank and waited for the vibrations to ease. Through the roar of the wind, Whisker made out a faint *twang*. He looked down in terror to see the strands of the footrope fraying and breaking away. With a second *twang,* the footrope tore apart.

Whisker shifted his weight to the handrail, but it was too late. With a loud *SNAP* ... *SNAP* ... sNAP ... the entire bridge split in two.

ELEVEN

At the End of the Rope

For one heart-stopping moment, Whisker hung suspended in thin air. Then, as the bridge collapsed beneath him, his terrified tail twisted around the handrail and his entire body plummeted down in a wide arc.

Planks of wood splintered off in all directions, crashing to the rocks below. Startled cries echoed from both sides of the ravine.

Petrified, Whisker held on for dear life as the upside-down rope swing hurtled back towards the massive ravine wall. The blurry shapes of shrubs and bushes raced towards him, filling his vision. Unable to slow his electrifying pace, he turned his back to the wall and braced himself for the impact.

CRUNCH!

Even with a padded backpack, Whisker felt like he'd been stampeded by a herd of obese elephants. Winded and woozy, he pulled himself closer to the cliff, as an avalanche of wood and rocks rattled past him. He waited for the crashing echoes to stop, and scrambled onto a small ledge halfway up the cliff.

'HE'S ALIVE ... *ALIVE* ... *ALIVE* ...' Horace cried from the opposite side of the ravine.

Whisker heard a cheer from his own side and looked up to see Smudge hovering next to him.

'Hi Smudge,' Whisker croaked. 'Have you got a spare set of wings … or perhaps a *rescue* rope?'

Smudge waved his arms in acknowledgement and zoomed up the cliff for a rope. Whisker was left to ponder his predicament.

'*Now* you ask for a rescue rope,' he mumbled to himself. 'You should have sent a rope across with Horace the first time!'

Within moments, the sturdy rope of the Pie Rats had dropped beside him and Whisker was clambering up. The onlookers at the top of the ravine shared Whisker's frustration.

'That's what we get for putting our faith in a century-old bridge,' the Captain muttered, pulling Whisker onto the plateau.

'I may have overestimated its strength,' Mr Tribble said, downcast. 'Silver plates are extremely heavy.'

Ruby gave Whisker a friendly nudge.

'At least I was right about Whisker's tail,' she grinned.

'Yes, yes,' the Captain agreed. 'We're all extremely relieved our young apprentice is still with us, especially after I pledged to keep him alive. But the fact remains that even Whisker's tail cannot get us across the ravine!'

'We could use the rescue rope,' Whisker said, holding up the end of it. 'It's long enough, and we know it's got the strength.'

'You fail to consider distance,' Mr Tribble pointed out. 'The opposite cliff top is well beyond our throwing range.'

'What about this?' Ruby said, removing a ball of string

from her backpack. 'It's extra strong, easy to throw, and Horace can use it to pull the rope across.'

'Give it a shot, Ruby,' Whisker encouraged. 'You've got a good Death Ball arm!'

Ruby unravelled the string and tied it to a small stone.

'CATCH THIS!' she shouted to Horace.

Horace crouched in a catching position as Ruby took a run up and hurled the stone into the air. It soared halfway across the ravine and dropped out of sight.

'Humph!' Ruby snorted, winding in the string.

She tried several more times, with no success. The rest of the crew fared no better. Smudge even tried flying across the ravine with the string in his arms, but the weight dragged him down. Horace grew restless, waiting for a catch that never came.

'GO AND FIND SOME FOOD,' the Captain shouted. 'THIS MIGHT TAKE A WHILE. I'LL SEND SMUDGE OVER TO KEEP YOU COMPANY.'

'YOU NEED A CANNON ... *CANNON* ... CANNON ...' Horace replied.

'Everything's warfare with Horace,' the Captain sighed.

'Warfare?' Whisker repeated. 'I think he's on to something.'

'Like what?' the Captain said puzzled.

Whisker was about to mention the hidden stash of dynamite when Eaton clapped his paws excitedly.

'What is it, Eaton,' Mr Tribble asked.

'At school,' Eaton said. 'You once told us about ancient inventions that shot stones at castles ...'

'A catapult!' Mr Tribble exclaimed. 'Of course! Why didn't I think of it sooner?'

'Genius idea, Eaton!' the Captain encouraged. 'But how

do we make one?'

'It's quite simple really,' Mr Tribble stated. 'My history students made a cherry-shooting catapult for last year's school fete. All that's required is thick rope, a bendy branch and a few large rocks.'

He took out his notebook and began sketching a design on a blank page. The others busied themselves dragging up lengths of rope from the collapsed bridge.

The Captain selected several large coils of un-frayed rope and laid them at Mr Tribble's feet. Mr Tribble nodded his approval and held up his design.

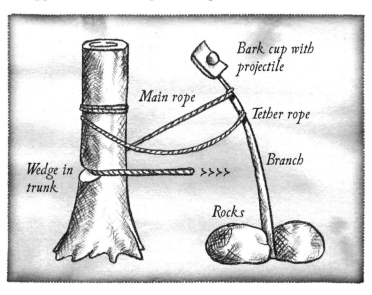

'This is a simple tree catapult,' he explained. 'A sturdy branch is secured between two rocks near the edge of the cliff. A rope is attached to the top of the branch and is pulled through a wedge in a tree trunk to tension the branch.'

'What's the second rope for?' the Captain asked.

'The tether rope is to ensure the branch stops before it reaches the vertical point,' Mr Tribble said. 'Otherwise the branch will continue in a downward arc, sending our projectile *into* the ravine, not *over* it.'

'A splendid design!' the Captain applauded. 'Now all we need is a large branch.'

'Or a small rubber tree,' Whisker said, pointing to a nearby sapling.

Ruby and the Captain helped Whisker chop down the rubber tree with their swords, while Mr Tribble and Eaton prepared the ropes. Horace lost interest watching from afar and wandered off with Smudge in search of jungle food.

Under Mr Tribble's guidance, the Pie Rats assembled their makeshift catapult. A round rock was attached to Ruby's string and positioned at the top of the sapling. The Captain handed Eaton his black scissor sword.

'Do you think you can handle one of these?' he asked politely.

Eaton looked hesitant.

'For Ratbeard's sake!' the Captain groaned, 'You're fighting a piece of *rope*. One hard chop is all you need.'

Eaton reluctantly took the sword and the Pie Rats positioned themselves along the rope.

'Where's that good-for-nothing Horace?' Ruby asked, peering across the ravine.

Horace stepped out of the trees with an armful of strawberry guavas.

'HERE I AM … *AM* … *AM* …' he echoed. 'I'VE GOT DINNER … *DINNER* … *DINNER* …'

'I'll give *you* dinner!' Ruby snapped. 'Now pay attention.'

While Horace watched attentively, Whisker, Ruby, Mr Tribble and the Captain began hauling the rope through the groove in the tree, bending the sapling backwards.

'Keep going,' Mr Tribble panted. 'We need more tension.'

The tug-of-war team pulled harder and the sapling creaked and shuddered to a standstill.

'It won't go any further,' the Captain said, gritting his teeth. 'Not without Fred's assistance!'

'Cut her free, Eaton!' Mr Tribble cried.

Eaton raised the sword above his tiny head and swung it down with all his might.

With a *SNAP – THWANG – VROOSH* the catapult fired. Whisker watched in awe as the rock raced over the ravine, leaving a trail of brown string in its wake.

CRACKLE – RUSTLE – THUD! The rock plunged into the forest high above Horace's head.

'SHIVER ME SPLINTERS … *SPLINTERS … SPLINTERS …*' Horace exclaimed. 'DID YOU SEE THAT … *THAT … THAT …*'

'Of course we saw it!' Ruby yelled. 'Now go and fetch my rock.'

Horace stuck a piece of strawberry guava in his mouth and scurried off with Smudge. Ruby tied her end of the string to the rescue rope and waited, tapping her feet impatiently. Mr Tribble held up several short loops of rope.

'I took the liberty to prepare six safety harnesses, Captain,' he said. '– just in case.'

The Captain nodded. 'Smart thinking, Mr Tribble. I'll attach them to the rescue rope and tie the end to a tree.'

While Whisker helped the Captain secure the harnesses, Horace reappeared with the rock and the string.

'Start pulling, Horace!' Ruby shouted. 'As soon as you have the rope, tie it to the thickest tree you can find – and Horace, triple check your knots!'

'YES, YOUR ROYAL RUBYNESS … *RUBYNESS … RUBYNESS …*'

It was dusk when Whisker finally reached the opposite side of the ravine. He was the last Pie Rat to cross. The strong wind, steep incline, and afternoon drizzle meant crossing the expanse with one rope was a slow and tedious process. The safety harness saved him from falling at least twice.

'Welcome to the ritzy side of the ravine,' Horace said, handing Whisker a strawberry guava.

'Thanks,' Whisker puffed. 'I'm starving. My stomach wouldn't stop rumbling the whole way over.'

He plonked himself down on a wet rock and bit into the juicy fruit. His mouth filled with the sweet taste of passionfruit and strawberries.

'Divine!' he marvelled.

'There are plenty more if you're hungry,' Horace said, helping himself to another guava. 'I found a tree near the ruined guardhouse.'

'Guardhouse?' the Captain enquired.

'Yes,' Horace said. 'It's just up the mountain.'

'Which means the citadel must be close,' Mr Tribble thought aloud.

'The citadel is an adventure for tomorrow,' the Captain said wearily. 'For now, I suggest we find a suitable place to set up camp. Can you direct us to the guardhouse, Horace?'

'Err, Smudge can,' Horace answered coyly. 'I got a little lost …'

The Captain rose to his feet. 'Lead the way, Smudge.'

'What about the rope?' Mr Tribble fretted. 'Don't we need it to get the key down?'

'We'll have to make do with Ruby's string,' the Captain said, regretfully. 'The rope can stay here for our return journey.'

Ruby looked wary. 'I'd prefer if the rope hung *unseen* among the vines, just in case we're being followed …'

'Monkeys?' Horace gasped.

'I don't know,' Ruby said, lowering her voice. 'But I did hear something on the other side, and it wasn't Whisker's stomach.'

Whisker gulped and tried not to choke on his guava.

As drizzle turned to rain, Ruby released the tension on the rope until it dangled low into the ravine. Stealing one last anxious glance across the expanse, Whisker plunged into the jungle after his companions.

TWELVE

Leaves and Stone

Exhausted and wet, the Pie Rats arrived at the small guardhouse high up the mountainside. A large guava tree stood near the entrance, its fruit-filled branches dangling over the threshold. Wearily, the seven travellers piled inside.

The guardhouse was a single, modest sized room with no windows and a cobblestone floor. Its four high walls were mostly intact, though its wooden roof had long since perished. A stone archway stood at the entrance, providing sufficient shelter from the evening rain.

The Pie Rats set up a cosy camp under the archway and lit a fire on the doorstep. They were comforted to know they had four strong walls and a roaring fire between themselves and the creatures of the jungle.

Dinner was a second round of strawberry guavas. The Captain thought it best if they kept their second pie for a far more dire occasion. Horace decided to char-grill his guavas for a little variety.

'Cooked to perfection!' he exclaimed, removing a blackened guava from the end of a toasting stick. He speared the guava with his hook and began chomping away at its singed flesh.

'Do you want some?' he said offering Whisker a bite.

'No thanks,' Whisker said firmly. 'I prefer my guavas medium rare.'

Horace shrugged and continued munching.

The soft shuffle of paper drew Whisker's attention from the fire. He looked over his shoulder to see the Captain examining the Forgotten Map in the flickering light.

'It's a little soggy,' the Captain commented. 'But the heat should dry it out in no time. It's lucky we have a map canister, or the map would have turned to pulp by now.'

Whisker looked down at the small metal tube lying next to the Captain. A cork stopper was wedged in one end and the canister was covered in a waterproof tar coating.

'It's not *puddle-proof*,' the Captain joked. 'But at least the ink hasn't run on the map.'

Whisker looked back at the map and stared closely at the words of the riddle. The Captain was right. None of the letters had run or smudged. He was about to make a comment about waterproof ink his father had bought for outdoor circus posters when he noticed something odd about several words in the second verse. He wondered how he could have missed them before.

'Captain,' he said, intrigued. 'Take a look at this.'

He read the first two lines of the second verse:

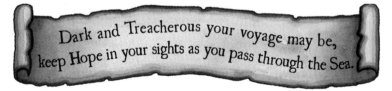

Dark and Treacherous your voyage may be, keep Hope in your sights as you pass through the Sea.

'You'd think a cartographer would be good at grammar,' Whisker remarked.

'Cart makers?' Horace said, joining the conversation.

'They don't know anything about grammar. All they know is where to stick the wheels!'

Ruby snorted loudly.

'What?' Horace said defensively. 'My dodgy uncle makes carts. I know all about them.'

'Cartographers don't make *carts*,' Mr Tribble explained. 'Cartographers make *maps*.'

'Oh,' Horace murmured. 'I knew that …'

Mr Tribble stood up and peered over the Captain's shoulder. 'What are we looking at?'

'A few misplaced capitals,' Whisker replied. 'Look at the words *Treacherous, Hope* and *Sea*.'

Mr Tribble adjusted his glasses. 'Are you sure they're misplaced? Cartographers are usually very thorough.'

The rest of the Pie Rats gathered around with interest. Eaton pointed to the rocky lagoon on the Island of Destiny.

'The *Treacherous Sea*,' the Captain read. 'Of course. It's a place name. Hence the capitals. The riddle is warning us about the dangers of the voyage through the Treacherous Sea.'

'I thought the danger was obvious,' Horace argued. 'Just look at all those rocks!'

'Maybe,' Whisker pondered. 'But there's more to it than that …' He thought back to the evening he'd run into Rat Bait, the former guardian of the map, and recalled the discussion that took place. 'Rat Bait mentioned a mysterious sea creature patrolling the island. The riddle says to *keep Hope in our sights*. Hope has a capital 'H' so it could be a place name like the Treacherous Sea.'

'A safe place to anchor to avoid the creature,' the Captain suggested, 'though I can't see *Hope* written anywhere on the map.'

'We're missing part of the map,' Ruby stated. 'And I'll bet a bunch of gold bananas that *Hope* has something to do with the key … what do you say Horace?'

Horace shook his head. 'I'm done making bets for the week, especially when it comes to food.'

None of the others had any better theories and decided it was unwise to bet against Ruby.

'I suspect we'll find *Hope* written on the bottom of the key,' the Captain yawned. 'But for now, I suggest we all get some sleep. We leave for the citadel at first light.'

With their thoughts focused on the mysterious key, the Pie Rats curled up around the fire and drifted off to sleep. Smudge kept watch at the entrance, just in case the marmosets were crazy enough to catapult themselves over the ravine.

The sun hovered low in a hazy sky. Smoke from the smouldering fire merged with the early morning mist.

Refreshed but achy from his rope bridge adventure, Whisker pulled himself to his feet. Horace stood nearby, surveying a pile of guavas.

'Another beautiful day in paradise,' he said cheerfully. 'What's it to be? Strawberry guavas covered in dew or strawberry guavas covered in ash?'

'Dew,' Whisker grunted.

'Good choice,' Horace agreed. 'That will be seven servings of dew-covered guavas coming up!'

'Oh, how I miss Fred's cooking,' Ruby muttered. 'What I'd give for a slice of Red Berry Combo pie right now.'

She glanced down at Mr Tribble's open backpack where the second pie sat, covered in long, stringy roots. Smudge attempted to sneak his way inside.

'Shoo fly!' Mr Tribble squeaked, hurriedly closing the bag. 'There is to be no sniffing, nibbling or gnawing the pie until we have located the key – Captain's orders!'

'Speaking of the Captain,' Whisker said looking around, 'has anyone seen him this morning?'

Smudge pointed up the mountain.

'No way!' Ruby exploded. 'He left without us?'

'He did say *first light*,' Whisker said.

Smudge shook his head.

'Kidnapped by drop bears?' Horace gasped.

Smudge threw his arms in the air as if to say *enough with the drop bears!*

'Well, where is he?' Ruby asked, with growing concern.

Smudge rubbed his stomach with one arm and pretended he was feeding himself with another.

'Eating?' Horace said puzzled.

'Not eating,' the Captain laughed, stepping out of the mist. 'Finding something *other* than guavas for breakfast.' Under each arm he carried an oblong yellow fruit.

'Mountain paw paws,' Whisker said, recognising them immediately. 'Nutritious!'

'Oooh *nutritious*!' Horace repeated. 'Too good for strawberry guavas are we, Whisker?'

'Uh, no,' Whisker said, taken aback. 'Mountain paw paws are a little sour on their own, but if we scoop out the seeds and stuff them with strawberry guavas they'll taste nearly as good as a berry pie.'

Horace twirled his hook in the air. 'Well aren't you the fancy pants chef! Fred had better watch his back.'

'I take it you're happy with your ash-covered guava, Horace?' the Captain said gruffly.

'Oh no!' Horace babbled. 'On the contrary, I would love one of Whisker's paw paw pie ... thingies.'

'Of course you would,' the Captain said with a bemused chuckle. 'You're never one to miss out!' He cut one of the paw paws in half with his sword. 'I had intended to bring back some jungle berries but the bush had been freshly raided.'

'Raided?' Horace gasped. 'By who? Monkeys?'

'I'm not sure,' the Captain said quietly. 'But the paw paw tree was left untouched ...'

'Marmosets *love* paw paws,' Whisker said thoughtfully. 'I saw platters and platters of them during the victory feast.'

'So that rules out the monkeys,' the Captain surmised.

'Perhaps the berry thief is nothing more than a harmless bird?' Mr Tribble suggested.

'Have you seen *any* birds since we've been on this

island?' Horace said, slightly panicked.

Mr Tribble pondered, 'Now that I come to think of it, no ...'

There was a short silence.

'So what's the big problem?' Ruby said, shrugging her shoulders. 'They're just berries. I doubt the thief eats keys.'

The Pie Rats agreed that Ruby had a good point. One by one they began to relax and turned to more important matters – the gourmet breakfast.

Well fed, the companions were in good spirits when they finally left the camp. In single file, they pushed their way through wet, waxy leaves and low-lying ferns and reached the outer wall of the mountain fortress in only a few minutes.

The citadel was constructed like a conventional castle, with four outer walls sloping up the mountain and a squat tower on each corner. A two-towered gatehouse stood at the entrance, leading to a large courtyard, where a dozen ruined buildings surrounded a large royal palace. Rising from the centre of the palace was a monumental round tower, spiralling high above the forest.

The Pie Rats stood in the entrance passage and marvelled at the sight before them. The mighty tower stood proud and strong among the crumbling ruins of the courtyard. Strangler figs, purple-flowered bougainvillea and other leafy vines covered its surface, transforming the cold stones into a tapestry of living colour.

'Purple ... the colour of kings,' Mr Tribble gasped. 'The jungle has reclaimed its throne!'

Remarkable as it was, the beauty of the tower was almost overshadowed by the eerie silence that hung in the air. No one dared to speak above a whisper.

'Who needs a rope with all those vines to climb?' Ruby muttered, stepping into the grassy courtyard.

'Stay together,' the Captain hissed. 'And watch where you're walking. I wouldn't be surprised if the whole place was booby trapped.'

Warily, the Pie Rats tiptoed across the courtyard towards the stone palace and reached a long flight of stairs leading up to an arched doorway. Whisker noticed a small symbol chiselled into the first step. The shape resembled an upward pointing arrowhead, commonly known as a *chevron.*

Mr Tribble took out his notebook and quickly copied it down.

'*Up* we go,' he said, shutting the book.

The jungle adventurers ascended the stairs. Enormous stone chimpanzees crouched on pedestals on either side of the staircase. Lush, green moss covered their weathered heads and torsos. They stared out at the approaching intruders with vacant stone eyes.

'Hardly friendly …' Horace whispered, stopping to examine one.

'Keep going,' the Captain said in a low growl. 'Statues carry terrible secrets from the past.'

Horace jumped back from the statue and scurried up the stairs.

At the top of the staircase the Pie Rats reached a small landing covered in black mould and dried leaves. Whisker felt a deep groove under his toes and curiously brushed the leaves aside with his foot. He looked down to see several small letters carved into the stone.

'Mr Tribble,' he whispered.

Mr Tribble didn't respond. He was lost in his thoughts, staring up at the palace wall.

Whisker followed his gaze. Carved in the underside of the arched doorway was a second symbol. It was a circle with two vertical lines extending above it.

'Do you recognise the design?' Whisker asked.

Mr Tribble shook his head. 'It's not an Aladryan symbol I'm familiar with.'

'I think it's Freeforian,' Horace piped. 'I've seen symbols like that in the volcano caves back home.'

'Can you tell us its meaning?' the Captain asked.

'Err, no,' Horace replied, clueless. 'I thought it was just cave graffiti.'

Whisker lowered his head and peered through the archway. A dark tunnel led into the palace.

'*Up* the stairs and through the *tunnel*,' he said thoughtfully.

Mr Tribble nodded. 'The symbol does looks like a tunnel. It could be from an underground code system. I've heard they still exist in some parts of the world. The symbols are used as navigation tools to prevent miners from losing their way.'

'That would explain the symbol's appearance in a Freeforian cave,' the Captain added.

'What about these letters?' Whisker said, pointing to the carvings on the landing. 'They might offer an explanation.'

Ruby hurriedly swept the remaining leaves off the stone to reveal a string of chiselled letters. The letters formed words and the words formed a message:

WISDOM AND WEALTH BE THE KEYS TO THY THRONE

Ruby frowned. 'What's that mumbo jumbo supposed to mean?'

'Perhaps it's a fancy way of saying *welcome to my house*,' Horace suggested.

Mr Tribble looked doubtful. 'I think it's more of a royal philosophy. It may have once served as a reminder for anyone entering the palace.'

'A reminder of what?' Whisker enquired.

Mr Tribble thought for a moment and then offered an interpretation. 'These words may have reminded the ancient kings that *wisdom* and *wealth* were key requirements of their royalty.'

'How modest,' Horace murmured. 'They obviously didn't consider *humility* as one of their treasured virtues ...'

'Humility's overrated,' Ruby cut in. '*Courage* and *honour* are the noblest virtues.'

'You're forgetting *humour*,' Horace added. 'Without humour life is duller than watching a seven ton rock erode in the rain.'

'You are *both* missing the point,' the Captain said fervently. 'This inscription tells us that the maker of the Forgotten Map stood in this exact spot and read these exact words before he – or *she* came up with the riddle. Why else would they include references to *wisdom, riches* and a *throne* in the verses? It confirms our theory. The key is *definitely* hidden within this building.'

'I agree with you on the engraving, Captain,' Mr Tribble said, raising his eyes to the top of the archway, 'though I still don't see the relevance of the symbols.'

'The symbols may be coincidental,' the Captain considered. 'But there's no harm in keeping a record of them. I have a feeling we'll need every clue we can find once we reach the Island of Destiny.'

With a small nod, Mr Tribble opened his notebook and hurriedly sketched the second symbol on the page with the arrowhead. The rest of the crew filed into the dark passage and disappeared into the gloom of the palace.

Dark Passages

Eerie black shadows clung to the high walls of the passage like sleeping bats. Fallen stones and stagnant puddles covered the rough, stone floor. Silently, the Pie Rats pressed on, arriving at three arched doorways.

Eaton lit his lantern and flipped open its mirrored sides, bathing the entire passage in light.

'More symbols,' the Captain said, looking up.

On the underside of the stone arches were three different carved symbols.

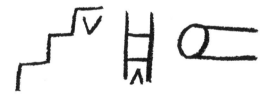

The doorway to the left led to a descending staircase. The symbol above it resembled three stairs falling to the left and a downward pointing chevron.

The centre doorway led to an ascending flight of stairs. Its symbol looked like a ladder or a frontal view of three stairs with an upward pointing chevron.

The right doorway was a continuation of the passage.

It carried a circular symbol with two horizontal lines extending to the right.

'It is my understanding that these symbols illustrate the direction of each passage,' Mr Tribble said, sketching the new symbols in his notebook.

'But how do we know which one to take?' Horace asked.

'I think that's obvious,' the Captain replied. 'The tower is up, so we take the middle doorway and head *up* the stairs.'

The companions climbed the steep steps of the middle passage until they reached a large pile of rubble. Collapsed stairs and broken stones lay in a jumbled heap. The pile extended from floor to ceiling, blocking the way forward.

'Rotten pies to rocks!' Horace exclaimed, kicking a stone with his foot. 'Ouch! We'll never budge these boulders.'

'Maybe there's another passage to the tower?' the Captain said, taking a step backwards.

'Wait,' Eaton squeaked, tipping his lantern upwards to illuminate the roof of the stairwell. Directly above the pile, several interlocking stones had fallen away. Eaton flipped the three mirrored sides of his lantern closed. A single bright beam projected through the hole to reveal a small room directly above the passage.

Ruby raced up the pile of rubble and stuck her head through the hole.

'Jackpot!' she exclaimed, pulling herself through. 'Come and take a look.'

Smudge buzzed his wings excitedly and followed after her. Horace and Whisker leapt up the rocks like two mountain goats.

'I can't quite reach the hole,' Horace said, standing on

his toes. 'I wouldn't usually ask, but …'

'You want a boost?' Whisker said. 'Sure thing.'

Whisker cupped his paws together and Horace climbed up.

'Come on, short stuff,' Ruby laughed, pulling Horace through the hole. 'I've found you a high chair!'

Whisker hoisted himself up and helped the rest of the crew into a rectangular waiting room. Small doorways stood at either end. There was enough light shining through the hole for Whisker to make out the symbols.

The doorway closest to the hole carried a symbol of three descending stairs. Whisker guessed this doorway led to the blocked stairwell.

The furthest doorway was bathed in a pale green light. The symbol chiselled into the underside of its arch was neither a tunnel nor a set of stairs. It was a five-fingered paw print.

Mr Tribble pointed to the paw and gasped, 'That symbol! I've seen it before. It's the right paw of royalty. If it's carved here, the doorway must lead to …'

'The throne room!' Horace cried, dashing through the

archway. Excitedly, Whisker scampered after him, entering the green-tinged interior of a glorious chamber.

The throne room was no ordinary room. It was the very heart of the citadel. Its circular wall rose up and up to the highest point of the stone tower. Small stairs jutted out from the stonework to form a narrow staircase spiralling up the wall.

Whisker immediately understood the reason for the strange green light. Dozens of small windows dotted the walls of the tower. Creepers and jungle vines covered the window openings, concealing the throne room from the world outside. Where the morning sun penetrated the dense foliage, evergreen leaves shone like stained glass shards on a moonlit night.

In the centre of the ancient room stood an enormous stone throne, supported by a pedestal with seven steps. The throne appeared to be carved from a single piece of white marble. Its high back was decorated with an engraved border of leaves, swirling around a crown. Two carved bananas served as armrests and the four legs of the throne resembled the limbs and paws of a giant ape.

Horace sat perched on the edge of the throne, waving his hook through the air like he was the pint-sized ruler of his own green universe.

'Bow before my majesty,' he proclaimed flamboyantly. 'And I will grant thee wishes three.'

Ruby shot Horace a look of exasperation . 'Kings don't grant three wishes, you marble-headed midget! *Genies* grant three wishes!'

'My majesty can do whatever my majesty wishes,' Horace replied indignantly.

'Your majesty can get his royal rear end off that throne

and help us find the key!' the Captain snapped.

'Aye aye, Captain,' Horace squealed, falling off the throne.

The Captain reached the top step of the plinth and laid the Forgotten Map on the marble seat. The rest of the crew gathered around him.

The Captain read:

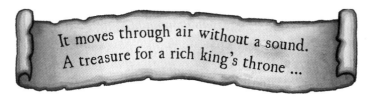

It moves through air without a sound.
A treasure for a rich king's throne ...

'Here is our *throne*,' he stated, tapping a banana armrest. 'And above us is the *air*.'

Six heads looked heavenwards to the distant roof of the tower, barely visible above them. One blowfly ascended into the lofty green void to explore.

'Smudge will tell us if there's anything up there,' the Captain said confidently. 'It's a long way to climb on a wild key-chase.'

'At least we have stairs,' Ruby pointed out.

'*Crumbling* stairs with *no handrail*,' Mr Tribble added sceptically.

'There are plenty of vines to grip on to,' the Captain noted. 'It's the lack of light I'm worried about.'

Eaton passed his lantern to the Captain.

The Captain smiled. 'Thank you, Eaton. That should solve our problem.'

Smudge quickly returned from his aerial exploration.

'And?' Horace asked in anticipation.

Smudge used three arms to form a circle in the air. He

thrust his fourth arm through the centre of the circle and gave it a sharp twist to the right.

'A key in a key hole!' Horace exclaimed. 'The key *must* be here!'

Smudge nodded and stuck four arms into the air.

'At the very top of the tower,' the Captain interpreted.

'Good,' Ruby said, removing a candy cane from her backpack. 'The walls slope inwards. The higher the key is, the easier it will be to reach.'

The Captain put his paw on Whisker's shoulder. 'Perhaps we should let our master climber retrieve the key?'

'We're a team!' Ruby said bluntly, clearly not wanting to miss out. 'Aren't we, Whisker?'

'Sure, Ruby,' Whisker replied, trying not to upset her.

'And I'm the third musketeer!' Horace piped. 'It's all for one and one of these tasty candy canes for me!' He grabbed a second candy cane from Ruby's backpack.

'You lick it, you lose it!' Ruby snapped.

Horace moved the candy cane away from his mouth and Ruby handed the third candy cane to Whisker.

'Take the string, too,' the Captain advised. 'There are no safety nets this time.'

Ruby pulled out the ball of string and hooked it on her belt.

'You're the lantern boy, Horace,' she ordered. 'Make sure we have enough light at all times. Widen the beam if you have to – and make sure you keep up!'

Mr Tribble pointed to the key-shaped hole on the map. 'Now remember what you're looking for. A three-toothed key, presumably made from a dense metal.'

'Yeah, yeah,' Horace mumbled, fiddling with the mirrors on the lantern. 'We've all seen keys before.'

Ruby didn't respond. She was already halfway to the stairs. Whisker took one last look at the map and scampered after her.

The three rats ascended the stairs at a brisk pace. Ruby led the way. Whisker stayed a safe distance behind her and Horace trailed at the rear, counting steps in a sing-song whisper. Smudge buzzed around the three rats, occasionally pointing out a cracked stair or a potential tripping hazard.

As Whisker climbed higher, he felt his chest pounding with excitement. It wasn't the key that set his heart racing, and it wasn't the treasure. It was the thought of his parents and sister. With every step he felt himself drawing closer to them. He imagined he was a pilgrim climbing to the top of a sacred mountain where the answer to one question awaited him – *Where are they?* He struggled to remain focused.

Get a grip, he told himself. *There is no sacred mountain. There's only a tower and a key. The key leads to a treasure. The treasure leads to … something.* All he could do was hope. He thought about the engraving on the palace step. *Wisdom and wealth …* What if *wisdom* and *wealth* were the secret treasures? Could wisdom find his family? Could wealth buy his answer? What if he had to choose …?

A loud shout from Ruby interrupted Whisker's thoughts.

'LOOK!' she cried, raising her candy cane into the air. 'Up there!'

Whisker stopped and stared. High above him, and dangling from the end of a rusty chain, hung a golden key. It shimmered like a distant star in the light of the lantern.

The rats hurried higher, eager to reach their prize. The

walls sloped inwards as the roof of the tower came into view. The Captain and the mice were now distant specks far below.

Whisker drew level with the key. It hovered silently in the air, begging to be touched.

'The King's Key,' he marvelled.

Ruby tried to reach the key with the end of the candy cane. Even with her arm fully extended, the key was well beyond reach.

'We need to go higher,' Horace puffed, reaching the two rats. 'We can reel in the chain from a step closer to the roof.'

'We can't!' Ruby said in frustration. 'The stairs end here.'

'Oh,' Horace said, looking up at the stair-less wall. 'It's good we have a grappling hook.'

Ruby gave him a rare smile. 'Good thinking, Horace. I knew there was a reason we brought you along.'

Horace and Whisker handed Ruby their candy canes and she began tying them together with the string. While he waited, Whisker examined the chain more closely. It was fastened to a round keystone in the centre of the roof. The bottom of the chain joined a gold ring, looping through a small hole in the handle of the key. Whisker saw no visible joins in any of the links.

'The key and the chain are fused together,' he said, perplexed.

'Nothing a few hard tugs won't fix,' Ruby muttered, unconcerned. 'One of those rusty links is sure to give way.' She held up the grappling hook. 'I've plaited the string so it's triple strength. Once I've hooked the key, I'll need you boys to pull as hard as you can without falling down the stairs.'

'Alright,' Whisker agreed. 'But we'd better warn the Captain and the mice first. No one wants a rusty chain falling on their head.'

Smudge disappeared below to give the warning, Horace lowered his lantern and Whisker braced himself against the wall.

'Here goes!' Ruby cried, swinging the grappling hook behind her back.

She projected it forward, releasing her grip. The grappling hook curved in a wide arc across the tower, striking the key with a *CLINK*. Whisker saw the four golden teeth of the key flash in the lantern light as the key swung backwards.

The grappling hook slipped from its hold and tumbled down. There was a faint grinding sound followed by a *CRACK* as the grappling hook hit the wall. The three rats sighed with disappointment and pulled the hook onto the top step.

Ruby prepared for a second throw and swung the hook behind her.

'Wait for the key to stop moving,' Horace squeaked.

Ruby let out an impatient groan and lowered the rope.

Mesmerised, Whisker watched the key swing back and forth, slowing down with every pass. He heard the faint grinding sound again.

It must be the chain, he told himself.

Ruby grew restless and raised the grappling hook. Whisker continued to stare at the key, hypnotised by its rhythm. His whole body began to sway – back and forth, side to side. His eyes fixed on the golden teeth of the key. As they moved in front of him, he saw them transform into ancient symbols … letters … numbers – *Numbers!*

'WAIT!' Whisker yelled.

But it was too late. Ruby had thrown.

FOURTEEN

Keys to thy Throne

The grappling hook hurtled through the air, speeding towards the golden key. Whisker clawed desperately at the string, unable to get a hold – he had to stop it.

As the hook neared its target, Whisker felt the lumpy shape of a knot. With rough fibres tearing at his skin, he closed his fists and pulled. The grappling hook jerked to a halt in midair and fell. The key continued to sway peacefully at the end of the chain.

Whisker felt his tail tingle with relief. Ruby gave him a furious scowl.

'What on earth were you thinking?' she yelled. 'I would have hooked it!'

'I – know –' Whisker panted, trying to catch his breath.

'What?' Ruby fumed. 'You deliberately tried to stop me! What kind of arrogant, worm-ridden, glory-hungry apprentice do you think you are?'

Whisker was too shocked to respond.

'He's the worm-ridden type that just saved your life,' Horace said in Whisker's defence.

'Saved my life?' Ruby exclaimed. 'From what?'

Horace pointed his hook at the ceiling. 'Have you

151

looked up lately, Ruby?'

Ruby raised her eye. The ceiling appeared the same as it had two minutes ago, with one big exception. The keystone supporting the chain had dislodged from the roof and was precariously balanced between the surrounding stones. One small tug on the chain would send the keystone plummeting to the ground.

'That explains the grinding sound,' Ruby gasped.

'I'm no stonemason,' Horace said. 'But my other uncle, who's not a dodgy cart maker, is. And I know for a fact that removing a keystone from any dome or archway is a guaranteed way to bring down the roof quicker than it takes to say *shiver me timbers, the sky is falling!*'

Ruby gulped. 'I-I'm sorry, Whisker, I shouldn't have …'

'Forget it, Ruby,' Whisker said, cutting her off. 'I didn't give you much warning.'

'But how did you know it was a trap?' she asked.

Whisker pointed to the golden key.

'I counted the teeth,' he said. 'The key from the map has three teeth. This key has four.'

Ruby gave Horace a sideways glance.

'I know, I know,' he muttered. 'We should have listened to Tribble.'

'So where's the real key?' Ruby asked, peering around the tower.

Whisker shrugged. 'Who knows? But I'm not waiting here for an answer to fall from the sky!'

Without further discussion, Horace picked up the lantern, Ruby slung the grappling hook over her shoulder and Whisker led the way down the stairs – as gently as possible. He listened for further grinding sounds with every step, but all he heard was Horace counting backwards.

After an anxious descent, the three rats reached the bottom of the stairs to find the throne room deserted and their companions nowhere in sight.

'Psst! Over here,' Mr Tribble hissed.

'Where?' Horace said, baffled. 'I can't see anyone.'

'We're under the throne!' the Captain whispered, poking his head between two marble legs. 'Is it safe to come out?'

'Not exactly,' Horace replied. 'But the last place you want to be is under that throne!'

'Why?' Mr Tribble asked, refusing to budge.

Whisker heard a faint grinding sound far above him.

'RUN!' he yelled. 'NOW!'

Mr Tribble didn't wait for an explanation. He scurried out of his hiding spot and hurtled down the side of the plinth, dragging Eaton by his collar. The Captain scampered closely behind them. Smudge was gone in a flash.

Ruby, Horace and Whisker grabbed their backpacks and ran towards the waiting room as the grinding sound continued. One by one, they dashed through the doorway and headed for the hole in the floor.

Whisker was directly under the arch when he heard the Captain cry out, 'The map! The map! The map is still on the throne!'

Whisker was typically a cautious character, but in the heat of the moment his caution was overwhelmed by a more powerful emotion – *desperation*. The map was his one hope. Without it, he had no chance of finding his family.

With a rush of blood to his tail, he tossed his backpack through the doorway and sprinted back into the throne room. Empty and eerie, it felt more like a burial tomb than a royal seat of kings. Whisker raced across the floor and leapt up the seven steps to the great white throne. The Forgotten Map lay unrolled on its marble seat.

As he scooped up the map in his arms, the ghostly green light of the chamber suddenly grew warmer.

Sunlight!

Whisker didn't look up. He didn't have time. He dived headfirst down the stairs – flying, tumbling, crashing over the steps as the entire ceiling of the tower tumbled onto the throne.

There was a deafening *CRACK* as the chair splintered into a thousand marble pieces. Rocks rained down, bouncing over the sides of the plinth. Whisker dragged himself along the floor, hoping and praying the next stone wasn't headed in his direction. He kept his head down and followed the sounds of voices crying out to him.

The voices grew louder.

He felt arms grab hold of his shirt and drag him through the doorway into the room beyond.

The rumbling stopped.

'What were you thinking?' the Captain roared. 'You could have been buried alive!'

Whisker raised his head. Ruby, Horace and the Captain stood over him.

'Sorry,' he said, letting his cautious side take over. 'I know it was reckless.'

'Reckless!' Horace exclaimed. 'That's an understatement if ever I heard one! If a cat has nine lives, you must have at least *ninety* – and you just used up half of them!'

'Don't expect us to attend your funeral, Whisker!' Ruby snapped, unable to hide her trembling voice. 'I – we all like you better alive. Do you hear?'

'Yes, Ruby,' Whisker said sheepishly. He extended the crumpled map to her. 'Peace offering?'

Ruby let out a long sigh and passed the map to the Captain. The Captain handed it straight back to Whisker.

'This is the second time you've rescued this map, Whisker,' he said, composing himself. 'So I'm entrusting you to look after it. Wherever you go, the map goes.'

Whisker nodded.

The Captain turned to Ruby and Horace. 'I take it one of you has the key hidden in a deep pocket?'

Ruby and Horace both looked at Whisker for an answer.

'Err, here's the thing, Captain …' Whisker began.

It took Whisker some time to explain the events of the tower. By the time he had finished, the dust had settled and the midday sun streamed majestically through the open roof of the throne room.

'So the golden key is under those stones?' Mr Tribble said, pointing to the pile of debris.

'Correct,' Whisker answered.

'And you said the key had *four* teeth?' Mr Tribble said. 'Not *three* teeth.'

'That's right,' Whisker said, unsure where Mr Tribble was headed.

'Four plus three equals seven.' Mr Tribble muttered. 'The plinth leading to the throne had seven steps …' He shrugged. 'Coincidence?'

'Maybe not,' Whisker said, straightening out the crumpled map. 'The riddle describes the key as *a treasure for a rich king's throne.* A golden key would normally be classed as treasure …'

'But it's the wrong key,' Horace groaned.

'So what else would a rich king consider as treasure?' Whisker asked.

Mr Tribble read from his notebook: '*Wisdom and wealth be the keys to thy throne.* If we take the inscription literally, there are two keys – one is wisdom, one is wealth. A *rich* king already has *wealth*, symbolised by the golden key …'

'Which means the *treasure* mentioned in the riddle on the map must be the three-toothed key known as *wisdom*!' Whisker exclaimed.

There was a nod of heads from the Pie Rats.

'According to the riddle,' Whisker continued, '*Wisdom is found in the shadows behind.* The true key isn't hanging in the glorious tower. It's hiding in the shadows waiting to be *uncovered.*'

'What shadows?' Horace asked. 'There are shadows everywhere. This place is one gloomy death-trap!'

'The shadows are *behind* something,' Whisker said. 'That could mean behind the tower, behind the palace or behind the throne …'

All eyes looked to where the throne had once stood.

'None of us thought to examine the back of the throne,' Mr Tribble sighed. 'I guess it's a bit late for that now.'

Eaton raised his paw.

'I err, had a look,' he said timidly, 'when we were hiding under the throne. I peeked out to see what was happening in the tower.'

'And did you see anything?' the Captain asked.

'Only carved leaves,' Eaton replied.

'That doesn't surprise me,' the Captain said, relieved.

'The throne is far too obvious a hiding spot. The maker of the map has gone to extraordinary lengths to conceal the key. I suggest we split up and search the citadel.'

'Where do we start?' Ruby asked eagerly.

'Mr Tribble and Eaton can join me on a hunt through the palace,' the Captain replied. 'The symbols above the doorways may provide us with a clue. Ruby, Whisker and Horace would be wise to examine the courtyard, and Smudge can do a flyover of the outer walls. Whistle if you see anything.'

'Aye aye, Captain,' Ruby and Whisker chanted in unison.

'Booby traps, here we come,' Horace added, with an obvious lack of enthusiasm.

Several hours later, three frustrated rats finished triple-checking the courtyard buildings.

'No key, no lunch, no afternoon siesta,' Horace groaned. 'Only stones, stones and more stones!'

Ruby wiped the water from her brow. 'Don't forget thorny vines and afternoon drizzle. My swords will rust before nightfall!'

'At least we've avoided the booby traps,' Whisker pointed out, trying to lighten the mood.

There was a faint whistle from inside the palace.

'That sounds more promising!' Horace exclaimed, taking off up the stairs.

Whisker and Ruby sprinted after him, following the main passage until they reached the three arched doorways.

'Which way?' Horace asked.

'Listen!' Ruby hissed.

A whistling sound echoed from the left doorway.

'Down!' Whisker said.

The rats descended the left staircase, fumbling their way through the darkness and tripping over loose stones. They came to two doorways and stopped.

'I can't hear the whistling,' Horace whispered, 'and it's too dark to see the symbols.'

'UNCLE!' Ruby shouted at the top of her lungs. 'CAN YOU HEAR ME?'

A faint reply drifted from the right doorway. Ruby chuckled to herself. 'Problem solved!'

The adventurers stumbled down a flight of worn, uneven steps, the air growing mustier as they continued.

'We should have brought a second lantern,' Horace grumbled, kicking something soft and squishy. 'I hope that was a mushroom and not a giant leech …'

'It's getting lighter,' Ruby said from further down the stairs. 'They must be close.'

The stairs spiralled to the left and stopped at the base of a small rusty gate. The gate was padlocked shut, but several of the bars had crumbled away and the rats easily squeezed through. Whisker looked up at the symbol above the gate. It was another paw – a *left* paw.

The gate led to a large cave-like room. Dozens of metal rings were attached to the rough stone walls. Eaton's lantern stood on a flat rock in the centre of the room. A long, deep gash ran across the centre of the rock.

'An executioner's stone,' Horace gulped. 'Something tells me we're not in a guest bedroom.'

'Hello there,' Mr Tribble said, turning to face the three rats. 'Welcome to the palace dungeon, where the left paw of despair watches over the sorry souls who will never again see the light of day.'

Whisker's tail dropped limply to the floor. 'How cheerful.'

'The left paw is also the symbol of the great brown bear,' Mr Tribble explained. 'And judging by the size of those rings, a large bear or two may have been chained up down here.'

'Where are they now?' Horace gasped. 'You don't think the bears could be –'

'– running wild in the jungle?' the Captain said, completing his sentence. 'No, Horace. Bears leave big tracks and we haven't seen or heard anything.'

'So why are we down here?' Ruby asked abruptly. 'Did you find the key?'

'I'm afraid not,' the Captain replied. 'But we did find this.' He pointed to a small anvil standing in a corner.

'An anvil?' Whisker said, puzzled.

'Not only an anvil,' Mr Tribble added excitedly, 'but the remnants of a coal forge and several blacksmith's tools.' He unfolded a dirty white cloth to reveal a hammer and a pair of tongs.

'Why would the apes use the dungeon for metalwork?' Whisker asked.

'They didn't,' Mr Tribble replied. 'But someone else did – more recently.' He led the rats over to the anvil. 'Take a look at the rocks.'

Whisker crouched down. The grimy rocks of the floor were dotted with small splotches of gold and brass and a clear substance that Whisker guessed was a by-product from the forging process.

'These rocks are evidence that our mysterious mapmaker used this secluded room to forge two keys,' Mr Tribble explained. 'One key was made from gold and the other from brass.' He patted Eaton on the head. 'Eaton also discovered several drips of paint on the anvil.'

'Which suggests the second key was painted to match the Forgotten Map,' Whisker thought aloud.

'That's all well and good,' Ruby said, 'but we still don't know *where* to find this key.'

Mr Tribble opened his notebook.

'I have successfully identified every symbol in the palace,' he stated. 'I'm afraid there is nothing to suggest the key is hidden within these walls.'

Whisker looked down at the open page. It was filled with navigational symbols and their meanings.

'Your list includes symbols for *water* and a *bridge*,' he commented. 'I wouldn't expect to find a river in the palace.'

'We discovered a small underground stream beneath the citadel,' Mr Tribble said. 'We reached it by taking the last doorway to the left. The bridge leads to a concealed rear entrance.'

'Like the Sally Port on Prison Island!' Horace exclaimed.

The Captain nodded.

'... *the shadows behind,*' Whisker pondered. 'Perhaps we should take another look at this secret entrance.'

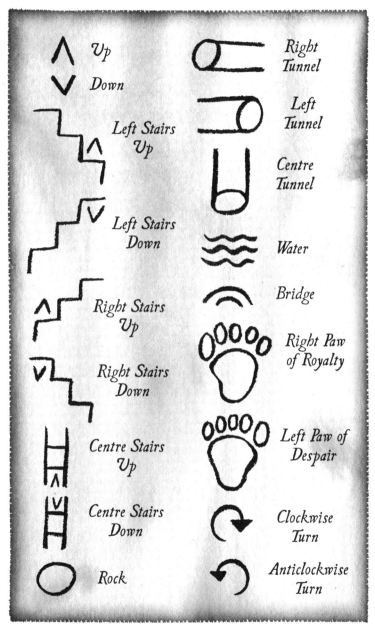

Up

Down

Left Stairs Up

Left Stairs Down

Right Stairs Up

Right Stairs Down

Centre Stairs Up

Centre Stairs Down

Rock

Right Tunnel

Left Tunnel

Centre Tunnel

Water

Bridge

Right Paw of Royalty

Left Paw of Despair

Clockwise Turn

Anticlockwise Turn

'What about Smudge?' Mr Tribble asked. 'Has anyone seen him recently?'

'Not since we left,' Horace answered. He probably found a rotten pile of paw paws to roll in!'

'I'm sure he'll turn up sooner or later,' the Captain said, unconcerned. 'Come on, this place is giving me an itchy neck.'

The crew followed the Captain past the executioner's stone. Horace snatched the white cloth from the anvil on his way out.

'Got a runny nose, Horace?' Ruby joked. 'Or simply fed up with using spiky leaves for toilet paper?'

Horace stuffed the cloth under his belt. 'If you really must know, Ruby, it's for a flaming torch – no more stubbing my toes in dark passages.'

'Well, keep it well away from me!' Ruby snapped. 'I know what you're like with fire.'

Bickering among themselves, the Pie Rats made their way up the dungeon stairs to the last junction. They took the left doorway and descended a steep path. The soft murmur of running water soon filled their ears.

The path opened out into a small cave, where a slow stream of water trickled from a rock in the wall. It playfully splashed across the floor before disappearing down a hole on the opposite side of the cave. The Pie Rats followed a rock bridge over the stream and continued up a carved flight of stairs.

The stairs levelled out into a short passage. Its stone floor dropped away to reveal a deep, round hole. Curved stone walls extended downwards into the darkness and upwards towards the sky. Looking up, Whisker could see a thick blanket of rain clouds high overhead.

'Argh me pastries!' Horace exclaimed. 'We're halfway down a well.'

'There weren't any wells in the courtyard,' Whisker recalled, trying to get his bearings. 'We must be beyond the citadel.'

'So how do we get out?' Ruby asked, fiddling with the grappling hook.

The Captain stuck his head over the edge and peered up.

'There are metal handles running up the wall,' he said. 'They look sturdy enough to climb, though a little slippery.'

Horace pushed past the Captain.

'I'll give it a shot,' he volunteered, 'Catch me if I fall!' Haphazardly, Horace climbed the side of the well, noisily scraping each rung with his hook. 'Nothing to it!' he yelled from the top. 'Come on up.'

One at a time, the Pie Rats clambered out of the well. Whisker reached the last rung to see the huge outer wall of the citadel towering above him. Several thick berry bushes grew nearby. Horace was already busy stuffing fruit into his mouth.

'Hey, save some for us!' Ruby scolded, rushing over. 'You've nearly eaten them all.'

'It wasn't me!' Horace spluttered. 'The bushes were half empty when I got here.'

'Maybe it was *him*,' the Captain said, pointing to a green speck flying towards them. Smudge buzzed around the Captain's head and landed on a branch. 'Where on earth have you been?' the Captain asked gruffly.

Smudge raised four arms as if to say *where on earth have YOU been?*

'Have you seen the key?' Ruby asked.

Smudge shook his head and pointed to a leaf.

'You've seen a leaf?' Ruby taunted. 'Well, good for you!'

Smudge took the leaf in his arms and began to shake it. Ruby ignored him and helped herself to a pawful of berries. Intrigued, Whisker watched Smudge closely. The agitated blowfly continued to shake the leaf while pointing into the jungle.

'You saw something moving through the leaves!' Whisker exclaimed.

Smudge nodded.

'Did you see what it was?' the Captain asked.

Smudge shook his head. Horace offered a guess.

'B-b-berry thief,' he stuttered, glancing warily over his shoulder. 'C-c-coming to g-g-get us ...'

The Pie Rats anxiously looked at one another.

'We don't have long until nightfall,' the Captain said in a low voice. 'I suggest we search for the key while we still have light and then set up camp in the palace.'

'I'm not searching in *there*,' Horace gasped, fixing his eyes on the darkening jungle.

'We'll stick to the wall,' the Captain said. 'The drizzle is easing, so it shouldn't take long to cover four sides.'

'As long as I can have my flaming torch,' Horace quibbled. 'Wild animals hate fire.'

He shakily wrapped the cloth around the end of a branch, drenched it in Eaton's lantern oil and lit it with a match. At first the torch did nothing but hiss in the drizzle, but with some gentle blowing, the flames began to burn steadily across the cloth. The fire seemed to revitalise Horace's spirits.

'Come on, Whisker!' he said cheerfully. 'I'm sure the

key is this way.'

Whisker followed Horace along the northern wall of the citadel while the others went east, disappearing around the corner of a squat tower. In the fading light, Whisker saw nothing he hadn't seen before – stacked stones, creeping vines, waxy leaves, sprawling shrubs.

The two rats came to a large pile of rocks where the entire wall had collapsed.

'I doubt we could dig through that,' Horace murmured.

'You search left,' Whisker said, 'and I'll search right. I'll see you on the other side.'

Horace gave Whisker a salute with his hook and disappeared behind the pile. Whisker followed the jungle side of the rocks and soon found himself surrounded by dense vegetation. He hastily drew his scissor sword and began hacking his way through the undergrowth. The citadel stones lay covered in a web of twisting vines and dense, broad leaves. If the key was there, he would never find it.

He came to a large tree, its bark rough and peeling.

SWISH.

He heard the sound and stopped. Puzzled, he scanned the forest floor for any signs of movement – the jungle was still and silent. Cautiously, he took another step into the undergrowth.

SWISH.

The sound came again. Whisker flattened himself against the trunk of the tree, his tail thudding anxiously against the bark.

Wind? he asked himself, looking up at the treetops. *It can't be. It's dead calm.*

SWISH.

He heard the sound a third time, clearer and louder. In rising fear, he lowered his eyes and peered into the shadowy twilight of the jungle. All he could see were green leaves and grey stones. His heart began to pound.

SWISH.

The sound was right in front of him now and, with a flicker of movement, it finally took shape. Astonished, Whisker rubbed his eyes.

'It can't be,' he gasped. 'It's impossible.'

Suspended in midair, and moving towards him like a ghostly apparition, was the unmistakable shape of a three-toothed key.

FIFTEEN

Appearances

Spellbound, Whisker could do nothing but stare as the key drifted closer. Leaves rippled and pulsed in its wake, changing colour from green to blue. Whisker willed it on. It was magical, it was mesmerising, it was ... *an illusion.*

Whisker saw the eyes before anything else – two tiny black pupils covered by yellow circles of skin. They darted in different directions, fixing and focusing on their surrounds.

Next he saw the horns – three stick-like shafts protruding from the creature's nose and head.

Finally the body materialised in front of him, long and scaly, with patches of green, grey and blue – the perfect jungle camouflage. Its reptilian tail coiled behind it in an emerald spiral, its four legs crept stealthily across the forest floor.

SWISH.

Attached to a fine chain around the creature's neck, dangled the King's Key.

Whisker raised his sword and the words of the riddle flashed through his mind ... *its guard appears as leaves and stone ...*

What a fool I have been! he thought. *The guard is not the leaves and stone of the jungle, it is the creature that takes their appearance: the three-horned chameleon!*

The green guardian stopped in its tracks and eyed Whisker suspiciously. Whisker's tail began to spasm.

Don't panic, he told himself. *It could be friendly. Just hold your ground and hold onto your sword.*

The chameleon opened his mouth, as if to yawn. Before Whisker knew what was happening a sticky tongue shot out and wrenched the sword from his paws. The chameleon spat the sword into the bushes and lowered its horns.

'Time to panic,' Whisker gulped.

The chameleon leapt into action, charging forward. Defenceless, Whisker grabbed hold of a vine and pulled himself up the trunk of the tree. The chameleon was right behind him. Its tong-like feet gripped the rough bark with ease and in moments it had reached him.

Whisker abandoned his vertical escape and leapt from the tree into a small bush. Prickly burs dug into his fur, but the leafy branches broke his fall. The chameleon turned itself around and scurried to the ground.

In a frenzy, Whisker burst from the branches, almost tripping over his scissor sword. He scooped up the slimy object and took off in the direction of the citadel with the chameleon racing after him in hot pursuit.

The stone wall came into view and Whisker felt the chameleon's tongue catch his ankle. His leg came to an abrupt halt but his upper body kept moving, tumbling into a pile of dry leaves. His sword flew from his grasp and he rolled onto his back as the chameleon bore down on him.

There was a fiery flash to his right and a loud shout of

'AVAST, YE SCURVY REPTILE!'

At the sight of Horace's flaming torch, the chameleon recoiled in terror, turned on its heel and fled into the jungle.

'Come back, you cowardly chameleon!' Horace yelled, waving his torch through the air. 'We're having roast reptile for dinner!'

Stunned, Whisker lay motionless in the pile of leaves, staring up at his pint-sized saviour.

'Thanks,' he murmured.

Horace lowered the torch and extended his hook to Whisker.

'Having trouble with the natives?' he asked.

'Only one of them,' Whisker replied, pulling himself to his feet. 'Your mysterious berry thief.'

'He's more than a berry thief,' Horace said, with wide eyes. 'I saw what he was carrying. That's some lucky charm!'

Whisker moved his paw to his gold anchor pendant.

'The chameleon won't part with the key willingly,' he said. 'That I'm certain of.'

'We'd better find the Captain,' Horace said, staring into the jungle. 'The torch won't burn forever, and I can feel that scaly creature watching us.'

Whisker felt it, too. Swords raised, the two rats scurried along the stone wall as the eerie darkness of night closed in.

That evening, a mighty fire blazed in the centre of the throne room. Sparks and embers drifted up with the smoke through the high chimney that was once the royal tower. The Pie Rats had slashed many of the vines from the windows, allowing fresh air to be drawn into the space, feeding the flames. The sky overhead was clear and the night air of the jungle was warm. The fire wasn't for heating. It was for protection.

The companions sat on fallen stones, a comfortable distance from the fire, and pondered their predicament.

'Are you sure it was the correct key?' Mr Tribble asked, writing notes in his book.

'I think so,' Whisker replied. 'I didn't get a close look but it definitely had the same shape as the hole in the map.'

'How old was the chameleon?' the Captain enquired. 'The map was made many years ago.'

'It's not going to drop dead of old age, if that's what you're wondering,' Horace said. 'The key must have anti-ageing powers!'

Ruby snorted.

'What?' Horace shot back. 'Haven't you heard of the *fountain of youth*?'

'Of course,' Ruby said sarcastically. 'I saw it this afternoon when I was …'

'Ahem!' the Captain interrupted.

Ruby and Horace silently glared at each other.

'Scientifically speaking,' Mr Tribble said, 'it is more probable that the chameleon is a descendent of the original guardian and that the key has been passed down from generation to generation.'

'Lucky us for getting the grumpy grandson,' Horace muttered. 'Shouldn't he just hand over the key? We figured out the riddle.'

'I'm not sure it works like that,' the Captain said. 'It appears we're in the middle of a dangerous duel with the mapmaker. If we want the key badly enough we will have to outwit and outsmart his guardian.'

'Out*fighting* the chameleon sounds like a better idea,' Ruby said, polishing her swords. 'It's seven against one.'

'Hmm,' the Captain pondered. 'I doubt he'll show himself in the open again, and if we try to hunt him through the jungle, he'll be gone long before we even get close.'

'What about a trap?' Whisker suggested. 'The chameleon seemed rather curious, and I'm sure if we found the right bait …'

'Insects!' Horace exclaimed. 'Chameleons love insects!'

Smudge leapt off the Captain's shoulder and buzzed through an open window.

'Come back, Smudge!' Horace called after him. 'I didn't mean *you* … I was thinking of a big juicy cockroach!'

Smudge didn't return.

'We know the chameleon likes berries,' Whisker remarked.

'So does Horace,' Ruby said, rolling her eye. 'He stripped the bushes bare.'

'You ate your fair share!' Horace retorted. 'If anyone's to blame it's …'

'I wasn't thinking of *wild* berries,' Whisker cut in. 'I was thinking of the berries in our pie!'

'Red Berry Combo!' Horace gasped. 'That's our dinner!'

Mr Tribble reached his paw into his backpack and pulled out the second pie. He brushed several long roots off the pastry and placed it on a rock. Smudge suddenly reappeared.

'It does look rather delicious,' Mr Tribble considered, licking his lips. 'If we remove the top crust, the berry filling will be irresistible!'

'Alright,' the Captain agreed. 'It's worth a try. But what do we do when the chameleon starts eating?'

'We could wait for it to fall asleep,' Horace suggested. 'Lots of animals do that after a big meal.'

'We can't be certain,' Mr Tribble said. 'And besides, it will wake up in a flash when it feels twelve furry paws snatching at the key.'

Something Mr Tribble said triggered a memory in Whisker's mind. He picked up a shrivelled root from the floor and examined it closely.

'What if the chameleon can't feel a thing?' he thought aloud.

The rest of the crew turned to him, awaiting an explanation. Whisker held up the root.

'Pete's treacle medicine!' Horace exclaimed.

'Whisker's berry medicine, more like it!' the Captain laughed. 'I think we have our solution. The chameleon will be fast asleep and numb from horns to tail before he's even finished the pie!'

'We can dry the herbs by the fire and grind them into a powder with the stones,' Mr Tribble said excitedly.

'Um, there's one little problem,' Whisker said, walking over to the Captain's bag.

He pulled out a black eyeball seed and held it up with one paw, raising the root in the other.

'One of these herbs is to *numb the pain*,' he said, quoting Pete, 'and the other is for a *healing rush of energy*. Pete never told us which herb is which.'

The Captain shrugged and scratched his head.

'Pete mentioned *roots* before he mentioned *seeds*,' Mr Tribble recalled. 'And he also mentioned *numbing the pain* before *healing rush of energy.* Therefore, taking a sequential interpretation, the roots are more likely to be the numbing herb.'

'You've lost me there,' Horace responded. 'I would have said the eyeballs were the numbing herbs. When I think of roots I think of energy rising from the earth.'

'Why don't we do a little experiment?' Ruby proposed. 'Mr Tribble can eat a root and Horace can eat an eyeball. The first rodent to fall asleep is the winner.'

Mr Tribble looked horrified.

'What if one of us never wakes up?' he choked. 'We know the herbs work harmlessly together, but on their own ...'

The Captain glanced across at Eaton, busily refilling his lantern with oil.

'What do you think, Eaton?' he asked. 'You don't say much, but you're a bright little lad.'

'Me?' Eaton squeaked, looking up. 'W-well, Pete said equal quantities of each herb ...'

'There you have it!' the Captain cheered. 'From the mouths of mice – problem solved! We'll use *both* herbs in equal proportions. If my memory serves me correctly, we'll have approximately twenty minutes to steal the key before the chameleon wakes up in a raging frenzy.' Without waiting for further debate, the Captain began scattering eyeball seeds onto the warm stones near the fire.

'Twenty minutes,' Mr Tribble considered. 'That should give us sufficient time to get to the ravine ... if we run.'

'Relax,' Horace reassured him. 'It's all downhill. We'll be there in ten minutes tops!'

Mr Tribble gave Horace an unconvincing nod and picked up a pawful of roots from his bag.

'These roots are your responsibility, Horace,' he said,

laying them on a stone. 'Constant supervision is required to ensure they dry slowly and evenly. Turn them over every five minutes and make sure they never catch alight.'

'How uninspiring,' Horace yawned. 'I'll be here all night.' He glanced over his shoulder at Whisker. 'At least I'll have someone to talk to. Pull up a rock, Whisker. I know hours of campfire ghost stories you're going to love.'

'Whisker's busy right now,' Ruby blurted out.

'Am I?' Whisker said, confused.

'Yes you are!' Ruby snapped. 'You're busy with your, err … first sword fighting lesson, which means *I'm* busy instructing you and Horace will need to find someone else to listen to his ghost stories.'

Horace shook his hook at Ruby.

'I know what you're playing at, you vile vixen!' he taunted. 'You don't want Whisker to hear a certain ghost story about a pretty young rat and a white sheet …'

Ruby flushed red.

'I-I don't know what you're talking about,' she gabbled. 'Come on, Whisker, it's too distracting in here for a proper lesson.'

Ruby dragged Whisker towards the waiting room. Horace grinned, and then continued, 'So Eaton, have you heard the one about the vampire bat and the vicar …?'

SIXTEEN

Master Strikes

As intrigued as he was about Horace's white sheet story, Whisker decided it was best *not* to raise the subject, especially when Ruby was facing him with a sword in each paw.

'S-so where do we begin?' he asked, nervously drawing his own green scissor sword.

'We already know your tail has some talent,' Ruby said bluntly. 'But as for your paws, well, that's a different story.'

Whisker knew Ruby wasn't going to be the friendliest of tutors, and she definitely wasn't going to inflate his head with praise. But sword fighting wasn't about feeling good, it was about staying alive. Whisker raised his chin and prepared for whatever came his way.

'There are two rules in the training arena,' Ruby began. 'Rule one: *Listen* to what I say. Rule two: *Do* what I say. Is that understood?'

'Yes, ma'am,' Whisker replied.

'And don't call me *ma'am!*' she snapped. 'I'm not your mother.'

'S-sorry, *Ruby*,' Whisker said timidly.

She continued, 'Sword fighting in the Pie Rat tradition involves two basic types of manoeuvres – *guards* and *strikes. Guards* are fighting stances giving you defensive protection, as well as a range of attacking possibilities. *Strikes* are movements that lead from one guard to the next. They can be attacking blows or defensive blocks.'

Ruby placed one of her swords on the ground and grasped the second sword in both paws.

'There are four primary guards,' she explained. 'The first is called the *Plough Guard*. It is simple to master, but hard for your opponent to penetrate.' She moved her left foot in front of her and twisted her right foot ninety degrees. 'Take note of my stance,' she said. 'One foot forward, one foot back. It will give you the best stability. Twist your torso so your belt buckle faces your opponent.'

Whisker tried to mimic her stance.

'Lower your paws to your right hip,' she instructed, 'and angle the blade so it points at your opponent's neck.'

Whisker awkwardly followed her directions.

'Relax your arms!' Ruby hissed. 'You're too tense … and remember to breathe … stop waving your tail … bend your elbows … move your arms closer to your body …'

Whisker felt like a marionette puppet on a bumpy cart ride. *You can do this*, he told himself. *Just focus your mind, listen and follow.* He took a deep breath and tried to relax. His tail stopped moving and his shoulders loosened. Maintaining his composure, he focused on Ruby and moved into position.

'Much better,' Ruby said. 'You're officially in the Plough Guard stance. From here, there are a number of strikes you can utilise, depending on your opponent's actions. Guard two is the *Roof Guard*.'

Ruby moved her feet closer together and raised the handle of her sword to her left shoulder. The blade of the sword extended vertically above her head, tipping back slightly. Whisker followed her closely, copying her every move. Ruby looked him up and down and nodded.

'The Roof Guard, like most guards, can be assumed on either side of the body,' she explained, changing position.

Whisker mirrored her with lightning speed and was in a reverse Roof Guard almost before she was. Blessed with quick reflexes, Whisker was determined to get every move right. He hoped Ruby could tell the difference between a keen student and an arrogant show-off.

Ruby glared back at him and mouthed something that looked remarkably like *arrogant show-off.*

'*Ox Guard,*' she snapped, raising her rear elbow. She lowered her blade to shoulder height and pointed it horizontally at Whisker. Whisker assumed the stance and the two combatants faced each other like angry oxen, horns raised, ready to charge.

'The last guard is the *Fool's Guard,*' Ruby explained. 'Rumour has it, it was named after a certain *fool* in our crew ...'

'Hey, I heard that!' cried a voice from the throne room. 'I'll have you know I have a famous move named after me and it's not the Fool's Guard. It's a skilful manoeuvre called the *Horace Shuffle!*'

Ruby rolled her eye. Whisker couldn't help but smile. The tension in the air immediately lifted.

'The Fool's Guard gives the *appearance* of vulnerability,' she continued, lowering the sword so the blade almost touched the ground. 'Your opponent will consider you a fool for leaving yourself wide open and rush in to attack. When they do ...' Before Whisker knew what was happening, Ruby thrust her sword upwards and took a swipe at an invisible foe. '… you'll be ready.'

'The *attacker* is the fool,' Whisker muttered to himself.

'The key to any fight is to find the *flow* of the battle and control it,' Ruby said calmly. 'Foresee a move before it happens and act decisively. As all good Pie Rats say, the best *defence* is good *offence.*'

'I'll try to remember that,' Whisker said.

'Control only comes with practice and experience,' Ruby added. 'There are many moves I can teach you but the four guards, together with the five Master Strikes, will give you a solid fighting foundation. Are you up for some sparring?'

'Sure,' Whisker said, growing in confidence. 'Anything beats dried herbs and ghost stories.'

'I can still hear you!' Horace yelped.

Ruby ignored Horace and began to explain, 'The five Master Strikes are: *The Strike of Wrath* …' She raised the sword above her head and swung it straight down, stopping the blade only millimetres from Whisker's head.

Whisker gulped. With a wink, Ruby raised the sword to her right shoulder.

'*The Crooked Strike* …' She curved the blade downwards in an arc across her body, ending the movement when the blade reached her lower left side.

'*The Cross Strike* …' Ruby began the strike from her shoulder, took a step forward and twisted her hips. The blade crossed horizontally in front of her face, with the tip pointing directly at Whisker's nose.

Whisker shuffled back.

'*The Squinting Strike* …' Ruby repeated her actions from the previous strike but ended the motion with a downward thrust to the right side of Whisker's neck.

Whisker shuffled back even further.

'And finally, *The Scalp Strike ...*' Ruby raised both paws high, stepped off line and thrust the sword in the direction of Whisker's scalp.

Whisker stared cross-eyed at the tip of the sword and thanked his lucky stars he'd taken two steps backwards.

'What do you think?' Ruby asked, lowering the blade.

'I-I'm glad I'm on your side,' Whisker stammered. 'I doubt I'd have much of a head left in a real fight!'

'The Master Strikes are designed to *threaten* your opponent,' Ruby said lowering her voice, 'not necessarily *kill* them. A good fighter will know exactly where their blade will end up. Experience will teach you about perception, timing and distance – three things that will save your life as well as giving you the power to *spare* lives.'

Whisker sighed. There was one question he'd avoided asking the entire time he'd been on the *Apple Pie*. It was a question he could no longer ignore. Before he went any further with his training, he had to know the answer.

'Ruby,' he asked slowly, 'What does it feel like to, err, k ...' He couldn't finish the question.

Ruby gave him one of her stone-cold stares and Whisker decided not to push his luck.

She bent down to pick up her second sword.

'I know what everyone thinks of me,' she muttered, 'and I don't blame them. I act a certain way – they assume certain things. But remember this, Whisker, appearances can be deceiving.' She paused. 'If you want an answer, you'll have to ask someone who knows. I'm a Pie Rat, not an assassin.'

Whisker smiled to himself. Ruby had given him the answer he wanted to hear.

'Let Horace believe what he wants,' Ruby added, quietly. 'He's easier to boss around that way. Fear is such a powerful thing! Come on. Help me pick out a couple of sturdy sticks for the training drill.'

Whisker followed Ruby through the throne room to a pile of dry branches near the fire. Horace was busy talking and laughing with Mr Tribble and the Captain. Horace was doing *all* the talking and *all* the laughing. Smudge dozed peacefully on a broken piece of marble.

'Where's Eaton?' Whisker asked, looking around.

Mr Tribble pointed up the wall. Through the smoke, Whisker could just make out the tiny figure of Eaton peering through a hole in a window. He was clutching his lantern in one paw.

'Eaton asked if he could survey the citadel from a safe height,' Mr Tribble said. 'He was rather concerned about the chameleon stalking us from the courtyard.'

'Are you sure he wasn't just spooked by a ghost story?' Whisker joked, selecting a straight stick from the pile.

'Rotten pies to snide remarks!' Horace huffed. 'Eaton loved my ghost stories. Especially the one about the white sheet and the ...'

'Can't stay and chat,' Ruby cut in, pulling Whisker out of the room. 'We've got heaps of training to cover.'

The sparring session was intense, to say the least. Whisker was glad they were fighting with sticks and not with swords. His mind struggled to piece together all the moves and combinations required to defend against Ruby and he was soon tender and sore from all the stabs and slashes he failed to block.

'You're improving,' Ruby remarked. 'But your mind is still too busy *thinking* about what moves to use. You should be *feeling* your way through each strike.'

'Give him a break,' Horace said, walking into the room. 'He's a million times better than I was in my first lesson.'

'That wouldn't be hard,' Ruby scoffed. 'By the way, aren't you supposed to be watching the herbs?'

'Tribble gave me an early mark,' Horace replied. 'I think my herbs got a little char-grilled ...'

'Just stay out of the way!' Ruby snapped. 'And if you mention a single word of *that* ghost story, I'll use you as a mannequin for decapitation practice – with real swords!'

Without protest, Horace shirked off into the shadows on the far side of the hole. Ruby gave Whisker a wink. 'I told you it was easy!'

Horace, however, didn't stay quiet for long.

'Err, permission to speak?' he piped, raising his hook in the air.

'What is it now, Horace?' Ruby groaned.

'I have a small suggestion for Whisker,' he replied. 'Combinations are easier to learn when you put them into a story. For example: The heroic Horace leapt off the *roof* and struck *wrathfully* at the *ploughman*.'

Ruby rolled her eye.

'Stories *can* work as learning tools,' she admitted. 'But unnecessary details will slow you down. The Captain taught me to use simple word associations to trigger my reflexes.'

She moved into a Fool's Guard position and explained, 'When I think of a *fool*, I think of someone who needs a few brain cells rammed into their *scalp*. 'She shot a quick glance at Horace and continued, 'An effective way to defend against someone in the Fool's Guard is by using the Scalp Strike. Another example is the word *ox*. I associate oxen with their horns, which are bent or *crooked*. So if someone is attacking me from an Ox Guard position …'

'Your defence would be a Crooked Strike!' Whisker exclaimed.

'Exactly,' Ruby said. 'And after a while you won't even need the associations. You'll simply know what moves to use and when to use them – with exceptions of course. It's important to be aware of your surroundings. A low ceiling height, a hole in the ground, sunlight in your eyes, and so on, can all influence a fight.'

'Don't forget props,' Horace added. 'A rotten guava to the face is a perfect way to throw your enemy off guard.'

'We're trying to stick to the basics,' Ruby huffed. 'That means two paws on the sword at all times, not picking up yesterday's dinner for a fruit salad food fight!'

'Relax,' Horace laughed. 'Whisker can use his tail!'

Whisker knew he had enough to focus on and filed Horace's suggestion in the back of his mind. His head soon swam with images of wrathful ploughmen, squinting fools and crooked horned oxen. Less and less of Ruby's blows penetrated his defences and he even came close to disarming Horace on one occasion.

'Tell me about the *Horace Shuffle*,' he panted, stopping for a drink.

'It's a cunning escape move,' Horace said proudly. 'But it only works if you're smaller than your opponent.'

'That's *never* a problem for you,' Ruby spluttered, trying not to choke on a mouthful of water.

'My size is my salvation!' Horace replied. 'I'll demonstrate for you.' He picked up Ruby's stick. 'Stand in front of me with your legs apart, Whisker.'

Whisker put down the flask and positioned himself in front of Horace. Horace took a few steps backwards and charged at Whisker with his stick raised.

Whisker waited until Horace was within range and swung down with a Crooked Strike. The stick passed through thin air. Horace had vanished.

Whisker looked down to see Horace sliding feet-first between his legs. With a cheeky grin, Horace gave Whisker's left foot a *WHACK* with his stick as he passed through. Whisker hopped on one foot, struggling not to fall over as Horace leapt to his feet and collided with the Captain.

The Captain wrenched the stick from Horace's paws and gave him a firm *WALLOP* on the backside.

'The *Horace Shuffle*!' he laughed, 'It's not much good if there's someone waiting on the other side!'

'It's still a stellar move,' Horace yelped. 'I got poor Whisker a good one! He thought I'd disappeared like a ghost – which reminds me, there's a great story about a white ...'

'Campfire stories are over for the night,' the Captain growled. 'We've finished drying and grinding the herbs, so it's time to get a few hours sleep before dawn.'

'Have you added the herbs to the pie yet?' Whisker asked, clutching his foot.

'Why? Do you want some?' the Captain asked, mildly amused.

'No. I'll recover,' Whisker moaned. 'I just wanted to make sure you put enough in.'

'Don't worry,' Mr Tribble said, stepping into the room. 'We added eight spoonfuls of the powdered herbs – four of each. That should be more than enough for a nice long nap. I'll take the remainder of the powder back to Pete.'

Eaton came into view carrying the red berry pie. The top crust had been removed to reveal a syrupy mix of raspberries, strawberries and cherries.

Horace's eyes lit up. Whisker's stomach rumbled.

'Don't even think about it,' the Captain murmured. 'And no, you can't have the top crust for supper.'

'Lucky chameleon,' Horace groaned.

'Speaking of the chameleon,' Whisker said, 'were there any signs of the elusive creature in the courtyard?'

'N-n-no,' Eaton squeaked in his usual timid voice. 'The courtyard *appeared* to be empty ...'

SEVENTEEN

The Guardian

Whisker slept restlessly that night. The image of the chameleon filled his dreams, stalking him through the jungle. He saw it in every leaf, in every stone. He couldn't escape.

He was running ... tripping ... falling ... The chameleon stood over him, its yellow eyes fixed on his chest. Whisker reached for his sword – it was gone.

In desperation, he raised his paws in defence. They were red, stained with the juice of berries. His body felt numb. He couldn't move.

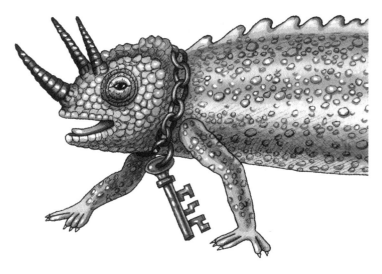

The creature crept closer, purposefully. It wanted something. It wanted his pendant.

Whisker couldn't speak. He couldn't scream …

The rain woke Whisker from his nightmare. It poured through the open roof of the tower, drenching him where he lay. The flames crackled and hissed. Steam filled the throne room. Thunder rumbled overhead.

The rain grew heavier and the Pie Rats scrambled for cover in the small waiting room. Six soggy rodents and a half-drowned blowfly watched the deluge bucketing down. In minutes the fire was no more than a smouldering pile of ash in the dim morning light.

'What's a rainforest without rain?' Mr Tribble yawned.

'More comfortable,' Ruby muttered, drying her swords on her vest.

Horace shook himself like a wet dog.

'It's lucky we left the pie in *this* room,' he said. 'The berries would have washed away.'

'If you hadn't eaten them first,' the Captain mused, wringing out his saturated hat.

Whisker said nothing. He was still shaken by his nightmare. He sat dripping in a corner, clutching his anchor pendant. Ruby wandered over to him and sat down. Whisker didn't move.

'What's up with you?' Ruby asked, giving him a nudge. 'You look like you've just seen a ghost.'

'I'm fine,' Whisker said, pulling himself together. 'But I wouldn't mention the *G* word with Horace around.'

'Good point,' Ruby acknowledged. 'Look – I didn't get a chance to tell you last night but you did … well, a pretty good job … you know, with the training.'

'Th-thanks,' Whisker stammered, unsure how to respond. 'You were pretty yourself – *pretty good* I-I mean ... a-as my instructor. You were pretty good as my instructor ...'

Whisker could feel the steam rising from his cheeks. He was *pretty* sure Ruby could see it. Luckily, Horace came bumbling to his aid.

'Come on, you two,' he said pulling them to their feet. 'We've got a chameleon to capture!'

The Pie Rats fastened their backpacks and clambered through the hole in the floor of the waiting room. With the light of Eaton's lantern and Horace's torch, they wound their way through the passages until they reached the underground bridge and followed the stairs to the well.

It was raining steadily outside. The pastry lid of the pie was placed over the berry filling and the Captain carefully slid the pie into Mr Tribble's backpack. It was fortunate the bags were lined with a thick waterproof coating.

The climb up the well was slippery and slow. By the time the Pie Rats had reached the top, they were once again sopping wet from nose to tail.

'It's now or never,' the Captain whispered. 'The chameleon feeds first thing in the morning. If we don't lay the bait soon, we may miss our opportunity.'

'Very well,' Mr Tribble murmured, removing the pie from his backpack. 'But we'll have to leave the lid on the pie to protect the filling.'

'Are you ready for your big performance, Horace?' the Captain asked.

'I'm always ready to perform!' Horace answered, grabbing the pie. He took a deep breath and began yelling at the top of his lungs, 'WHAT A SCRUMPTIOUS

BERRY PIE THIS IS! IT'S MOUTH-WATERINGLY MAGNIFICENT! IT'S BERRY-LICIOUSLY BRILLIANT! IT'S DIGESTIVELY DIVINE! I COULD EAT IT ALL MYSELF!'

'HEY!' Whisker shouted. 'What about the rest of us? We love berries too!'

'YES!' Ruby cheered. 'BERRIES ARE THE BEST!'

'GOOD GRACIOUS!' the Captain bellowed. 'We're going to need more berries than this to feed *everyone*. Gather 'round, crew, and see what you can find!'

Horace put the pie on the ground and began combing the nearest bush for berries. The others joined in. The bushes, as predicted, were empty.

'You gluttonous glutton, Horace!' Ruby exclaimed. 'You ate all the berries yesterday!'

'DID NOT!' Horace shouted, shaking his hook at her.

'Forget the berry bushes,' the Captain cried. 'There are strawberry guavas this way!' He scampered down the northern wall. 'HURRY!'

The Pie Rats dashed after the Captain, leaving the berry pie sitting under a bush. Smudge doubled back to the well to take up his position as lookout while the rest of the crew climbed through the hole in the wall to the courtyard.

Whisker pointed to a small building nearby.

'We can hide in there,' he whispered. 'It's still got half its roof on.'

The Pie Rats clambered into the small outhouse and found a dry spot to wait.

'Not a word!' the Captain hissed, glaring at Horace.

Horace plonked himself on the ground and began drawing in the dirt. The others leant against the wall, listening to the sound of falling rain and awaiting the return of Smudge. Time passed, the rain eased, but there was no sign of Smudge. Lightning flashed, the rain grew heavy – still no sign of Smudge.

Whisker pictured the pie turning into a pile of soggy pastry sludge and its precious syrup oozing out. He recalled the words of the Pie Rat code – *No pie shall be wasted.*

It's more than a waste, he thought to himself. *It's an absolute disaster.*

He was too busy dwelling on his disastrous vision to notice the rain slowing to a drizzle. Nor did he hear the faint buzz of wings until Smudge was inside the building.

'What news?' Horace cried, jumping to his feet.

Smudge tipped his head to one side and closed his eyes like he was sleeping. Mr Tribble clapped his paws together. 'It worked!'

'So far …' the Captain said warily. 'How long has the chameleon been asleep, Smudge?'

Smudge raised one arm in the air, lowered it and then raised another five.

'Fifteen minutes!' Horace gasped. 'What took you?'

Smudge pointed to a dark cloud outside as if to say, *you try flying in a thunderstorm*!

'Never mind,' the Captain said resolutely. 'Let's get moving. Every minute counts.'

The Captain led the procession of berry-lovers back through the courtyard. The drizzling had stopped completely by the time they reached the outer wall, and the jungle grew silent.

The Pie Rats crept closer to the bushes and drew their swords. The long green shape of the chameleon lay motionless on the ground. Its yellow eyes were closed, its scaly mouth was covered with red syrup and its horns protruded into the half-eaten pie. Whisker's nightmare flashed before his eyes.

It can't hurt you, he told himself, gripping his sword.

The Captain cautiously approached the creature and gave it a prod with his foot. It didn't stir. Mr Tribble bent down and wiped the drizzle from his glasses.

'This looks like our key,' he said, pointing to an object at the end of a chain. 'I can't make out the detail with all the mud, but the shape appears to be an exact match. Do you have the map, Whisker?'

'Yes,' Whisker replied, still keeping his distance. 'It's rolled up in my backpack.'

'There's no time to check,' the Captain said gruffly. 'Our mission is to get the key and get out of here.'

Horace and Ruby grabbed hold of the chain and tried to pull it over the chameleon's head. The chain caught in the folds of the skin beneath the creature's chin.

'It seems our guard has grown attached to his necklace,' Mr Tribble observed. 'You'll never get it off that way.'

'Try breaking the chain,' Whisker suggested.

Horace wedged his hook through one of the links and attempted to wrench it apart. His efforts were in vain.

'It's stronger than it looks,' he groaned. 'I doubt Fred could break these links apart.'

Whisker looked down at the sleeping chameleon and knew he must face his fears. He put his sword in his belt, picked up a heavy rock and lugged it towards the chameleon's head.

It won't feel a thing he said to himself. *It won't wake up.*

'W-what are you doing?' Horace asked in horror. 'You're not going to …?'

THUD!

Whisker dropped the rock to the ground. As the others watched, he slid the rock closer to the chameleon.

'Just like an executioner's stone,' he muttered, draping the chain over the rock. 'Without the severed heads of course. Now, who's our executioner?'

Ruby moved into position with her sword.

'Hold the key steady, Whisker,' she said. 'And someone grab the other end of the chain. I want it taut and secure.'

Whisker clasped the muddy key in both paws. Horace held the chain in place with his hook. A large metal fastening ring passed through the centre of the key, attaching it to the chain.

'Aim for the ring,' Whisker said, 'It looks weaker than the chain.'

'It's awfully close to your paws!' Horace gasped. 'What if ...'

'Relax,' Ruby said. 'Whisker won't be joining your one-pawed club!' She raised her sword and looked down at Whisker. 'After three. Ready? One ... two ... three ...'

WHOOSH – CHING!

Whisker felt a jolting vibration as Ruby's sword hit the ring. He looked down to see a large chink in the metal, but the ring held fast.

'Try again,' he said. 'Same spot.'

As Ruby prepared to swing, Whisker saw a flicker of movement out of the corner of his eye and jumped backwards in fright. Staring straight at him was the open eye of the chameleon.

'Putrid pastries!' Horace gasped, pulling his hook from the chain. 'It's awake!'

Ruby held her ground.

'Get the crew out of here, Uncle,' she hissed. 'Whisker and I will meet you at the ravine.'

No one moved.

'GO!' Ruby yelled.

The Captain grabbed the two terrified mice and pulled them away from the chameleon. Horace staggered backwards after them, not lifting his gaze from the awakening creature.

'Keep the chain steady, Whisker,' Ruby instructed, raising her sword.

Trying to ignore the eye staring at him, Whisker grabbed the key and pulled the chain over the rock. Ruby swung her sword down in a powerful arc.

CHING!

The gash in the metal widened but the ring remained intact. The chameleon began to stir. Its tail quivered, its legs flexed and its head swivelled to face Whisker.

'Hurry!' Whisker shouted as the chameleon tried to prod him with its horns.

'One more shot!' Ruby hissed, arching her sword above her head.

She swung her sword through the air and the blade rocketed down with pinpoint accuracy. At the last moment, the chameleon flinched and the key slipped from Whisker's paws.

CHING!

The sword made contact with the ring. Nothing happened – Ruby had missed her mark. The chameleon rose unsteadily to its feet and Whisker made a frantic grab for the key. He saw two deep grooves marking the side of the ring and knew it hung by a thread. Gripping the jagged teeth of the key, he tried pulling it free. The chain dug further into the chameleon's skin but failed to release.

Ruby stashed her sword and rushed to Whisker's aid as the chameleon took a wobbly step forward. She clutched the chain in both paws and swung herself onto the chameleon's back. Whisker heaved the key from below while Ruby tugged from above. The chameleon's front legs collapsed beneath it and it sprawled into the mud. Whisker rolled clear but refused to let go.

'Keep pulling!' Ruby shouted. 'I can feel it breaking.'

Whisker pulled harder – Ruby pulled harder still. With a mighty surge of energy, the chameleon found its strength. Its emerald skin turned black as it exploded into action. Like a panther pouncing on its prey, it hurtled head first into the bushes, dragging two unwelcome passengers with it.

EIGHTEEN

The Jungle Express

The chameleon thrashed its head from side to side as it charged through the undergrowth. Whisker, Still clutching the key, struggled to hold on as he was scraped through the mud. Ruby, battered by branches, flattened herself against the chameleon's back and clung on for dear life.

The chameleon leapt over a log and the chain swung upwards, pulling Whisker's body into the air. The chameleon descended, landing on a pile of stones, and Whisker plummeted down.

Ruby released one of her paws and made a frantic grab for Whisker's arm. She caught the back of his shirt and dragged him onto the chameleon's back. Together, the master swords-rat and the apprentice looped their fingers through the ring and held on tight. If they were going down, the key was coming with them.

The wild reptile continued to barge and crash its way through the dense vegetation of the jungle. Leaves and sticks smacked Whisker's face. Water sprayed in his eyes. Trees sped past him in a green blur. He wondered if the chameleon would ever run out of energy.

Ruby slid to one side as the chameleon ploughed

through a patch of ferns. Whisker twisted his tail around her leg to stop her falling. Seconds later, the chameleon veered to its right to avoid a lichen-covered rock and Ruby bounced into the air, crashing down on top of Whisker.

He let out a pained howl as the sharp tip of her sword pierced his leg.

'You'll live!' she shouted. 'Now hold on, cowboy, we're headed for the ravine!'

The chameleon increased its pace, scrambling down a steep bank of the mountain. Through gaps in the foliage, Whisker could see the sunlit cliffs of the ravine ahead.

'T-t-tell me it's not going to …' he stammered in panic.

Ruby didn't answer. She grabbed the ring with her second paw and began to twist.

'Help me!' she shouted,

Following Ruby's lead, Whisker twisted the ring in the opposite direction. With their efforts combined, the metal began to bend.

'We're nearly there!' Ruby exclaimed.

Whisker looked up. They were nearly *there* – the green canopy of the jungle had vanished and the rocky plateau of the cliff top stretched in front of them. The tight rope of the Pie Rats hung to their right, spanning the ravine from cliff to cliff.

Eight metres to the edge, he calculated.

To Whisker's horror, he realised the chameleon wasn't headed for the rope: it was headed for the bridge – the bridge that wasn't there.

Six metres.

'We've got time!' Ruby shouted. 'Keep trying.'

Whisker strained harder, his muscles cramping, his fingers turning white. The metal bent further; but not enough.

Four metres.

'Come on!' Ruby cried, refusing to give in.

Whisker twisted, heaved and tugged with every ounce of his strength, but it still wasn't enough.

Two metres.

'JUMP!' he screamed.

The chameleon skidded to a halt. Whisker and Ruby kept moving. There was a sharp *SNAP* as their bodies hurtled over the head of the chameleon.

Whisker saw three terrifying things at once: the edge of the cliff rising towards him, Ruby somersaulting downwards and the key spinning out of control through the air.

For a split second, time slowed down, and in that moment, a strange thought flashed through Whisker's mind: *Never touch a crooked fool's scalp.*

Time sped up. Whisker twisted his hips, flicked his tail in a wide arc over his shoulder and curved it down in front of him. Simultaneously, he extended his left paw downwards and thrust his right paw upwards. He felt a sharp tug on his left paw followed by a sharper tug on his right paw. Gritting his teeth, he hoped his aching fingers were strong enough to do their job.

His body stopped moving. Cautiously, he looked around. He was lying next to Ruby on the very edge of the ravine. His right paw gripped a large rock and his left paw clutched Ruby's arm. He could feel his tail dangling over the cliff, wrapped tightly around the key.

His prize was secure but there was still one problem. The furious chameleon towered over him. It narrowed its eyes, lowered its head and aimed its horns directly at his chest.

Whisker waited for the painful stab. There was a loud shout from the plateau and the chameleon whipped around to face the new threat.

Seizing his opportunity, Whisker staggered to his feet, pulling Ruby up with him, and his tail dragged the key onto the ledge. Horace stood several metres away, brandishing a flaming torch in one paw and a stick of unlit dynamite in his hook.

'Burn you brutish beast!' he cried, waving the torch at the chameleon. 'And if you touch my friends again, you'll be sucking on a sizzling stick of dynamite.'

The chameleon moved to its left, its eyes darting between Horace and the dense jungle. Horace stepped in its path, denying it an easy escape.

'Let it pass!' Whisker shouted. 'We have the key.'

Obediently, Horace lowered the torch and moved out of the reptile's way. The chameleon eyed him cautiously but refused to budge.

'W-what's it doing?' Horace stammered, raising the torch again.

As Whisker and Ruby watched, the Captain and the mice burst from the undergrowth, puffing hard. Smudge scrambled into the Captain's backpack when he saw the chameleon. The Captain pointed his sword at the creature and panted, 'Chameleon – here – but how? – behind us – a minute ago –'

Whisker saw the danger before the others, but it was Ruby who found the lungs to scream, 'BEHIND YOU! LOOK OUT!'

A green shape hurtled out of the jungle, knocking Eaton and Mr Tribble off their feet. The Captain dived out of the way, as a hornless chameleon charged across the plateau.

'Argh me pastries!' Horace gasped. 'The chameleon has a mate.'

The second chameleon fixed its yellow eyes on Whisker's tail and made a beeline for the key. Before Whisker could untangle the key from his tail, the chameleon's tongue shot out and caught hold of it – tail and all. Whisker jerked forward as the chameleon reeled him in.

Ruby ran to Whisker's aid but the horned chameleon battered her backwards with a flick of its tail. She crashed into Horace, sending the dynamite flying. There was a shower of sparks as the fuse spun through the flames of the torch, igniting on impact.

The hissing stick of dynamite hit the ground, only inches from the second chameleon. Oblivious to the danger, it continued to drag Whisker closer.

Whisker grabbed his tail with his paws to stop himself sliding. It was a *tail* versus *tongue* tug-of-war. And he was losing.

He heard thundering footsteps to his left and turned to see the first chameleon charging at him. There was only one direction he could go. He leapt towards the second chameleon and the end of his tail disappeared into its mouth. Three brown horns brushed past him, narrowly missing his head.

He watched helplessly as the chameleon's jaws closed shut. He held his breath and waited for the bite.

With an agonising CRUNCH, the chameleon's jaws stopped. Whisker exhaled with relief – the key lay wedged between its teeth.

'Catch!' Horace shouted, hurling Whisker the torch.

Whisker plucked the flaming torch from the air and

thrust it into the chameleon's mouth. There was a hiss of steaming saliva. The chameleon rolled its eyes and spat out Whisker's tail.

Whisker stumbled backwards, narrowly avoiding a second collision with the horned chameleon. Hastily, he unravelled the gooey key from his tail and shoved it deep into his pocket.

'Get going!' he yelled. 'I'll hold them off.'

He waved the torch in wide sweeps through the air as the rest of the Pie Rats scrambled for the rope. The stick of dynamite continued to sizzle behind the chameleons, its extra-long fuse already three-quarters burnt.

'Hurry!' Whisker shouted. 'We've got a *dead*line to meet.'

Mr Tribble fumbled with a safety harness.

'*Survival* before *safety*!' Ruby snapped, throwing the harness over the cliff. 'There's no time to climb!'

'So how do we get across?' Mr Tribble gasped.

Ruby thrust a sticky candy cane into his paws.

'Essential survival item,' she hissed.

Mr Tribble stared at the sugary object.

'W-what am I supposed to do with this?' he stammered.

The Captain grabbed Eaton under one arm and hooked Ruby's second candy cane over the rope.

'You hold on tight!' he cried, leaping off the cliff.

Eaton squealed in terror as they raced down the rope. In seconds they had reached the opposite side of the ravine and crash-landed into the catapult.

Whisker's torch began to smoulder. The chameleons crept closer, their fear dwindling.

'We have a problem!' Whisker coughed through the

smoke.

Mr Tribble froze on the edge of the cliff.

'You've got three seconds before I throw you off, Tribble,' Ruby shouted, hooking the candy cane over the rope. 'One ... two ...'

Mr Tribble clasped the stick.

'... three!' Ruby gave him a hard shove and he was gone. 'You're up next, Horace!' she yelled.

Horace looped his hook over the rope.

'No assistance necessary,' he panted. Ruby gave him a firm kick all the same, and he sped down the rope like a bullet.

Horace was almost at the opposite side when Whisker's torch went out completely. He hurled the smoking stump at the closest chameleon and ran for his life.

He could hear the clatter of chameleons behind him and the crackle of the fuse burning to its end, but his eyes were fixed on one thing: Ruby – she wasn't leaving without him. She stood on the edge of the cliff holding the last remaining candy cane in her paws with a look that said *get here at once, apprentice!*

Whisker wasn't one to disappoint. He scrambled over the rocks faster than a rat trying to outrun two killer chameleons and a ticking time bomb. In moments he'd reached the rope.

Whisker was muddy, smoky, soggy and dripping with chameleon spit. As he wrapped his filthy arm around Ruby's waist and leapt off the cliff, he hoped she'd forgive him for ruining her outfit.

The two rats rocketed down the rope. Whisker's heart pounded like a drum. The wind buffeted his cheeks, the crisp air stung his eyes. He was on a flying-fox ride on overdrive. Halfway down, he glanced over his shoulder to see the defeated chameleons disappear into the jungle. He turned back. The opposite cliff was right in front of him.

KABOOM ... KABOOM ... KABOOM ...

The stick of deadly dynamite exploded with volcanic intensity. Whisker and Ruby were thrown from the rope, somersaulting through the air onto the cliff top. Their bodies tumbled over slippery stones and came to rest in a leafy bush. No sooner had they landed, than a hailstorm of rubble peppered the cliff top.

'RUN!' Horace shouted.

Ruby was on her feet in an instant and sprinted after the escaping crew. Whisker untangled his foot from a branch and stumbled blindly into the jungle. Rocks slammed into tree trunks around him, sending shards of stone crashing through the dense layers of leaves. He ducked for cover behind a log and waited.

When the last flying projectile had come to a stop, he cautiously raised his head and looked around. He was alone. The distant drone of Horace counting backwards told him where to find his companions: the mountain stairs.

He rose to his feet, took a step through the undergrowth – and stopped. Something felt terribly wrong.

In rising dread, he stuck his paw in his pocket and double checked its contents. His fingers touched the jagged tooth of a key. He reached his arm over his shoulder and felt the map canister bulging from his backpack. The key and map were safe, but his feeling of unease remained.

What is it? he thought. *What did I see?*

Searching for clarity, he tried to recall the day he first crossed the ravine. He closed his eyes and pictured the cliff tops.

201

Ruby left the rope dangling into the ravine. Today we found it stretched tightly across ...

Whisker's chest grew tight. He began to run. He didn't know *who* and he didn't know *why*, but he knew he wasn't alone.

I have to warn the others, he thought with dire urgency.

He heard a *SNAP* to his right, glimpsed a bright flash of silver and, with a hard blow to the back of his head, everything went black.

Old Enemies

'Whisker! Whisker! Wake up!'

Whisker felt rough paws shaking his body. His mind slowly registered the sounds. He struggled to comprehend where he was or what had happened.

'They've taken it,' a voice cried.

Whisker forced his eyes open. The sunlight stung his eyes. His head pounded. Dazedly, he looked up. He was lying in the middle of the jungle. Ruby, Horace and Mr Tribble stood over him. Smudge circled overhead.

'The key's gone!' Horace cried.

Whisker slid his paw down his leg and touched his pocket. It was empty.

'Backpack …' he croaked.

The Captain came into view, holding the tattered remains of Whisker's backpack and an empty map canister.

'They have the map, too,' he said soberly, 'and your silver plates.'

'*Who?*' Whisker spluttered, trying to sit up.

'The Cat Fish!' Horace gasped. 'Prowler and Cleopatra. We came looking for you and found *them*.'

Whisker felt sick.

'You're lucky to be alive,' Mr Tribble said. 'If Horace hadn't scared them off with his dynamite, you ... well, we don't think about that.'

'B-but how did they find us?' Whisker stammered.

'Rat Bait, I'm guessing,' the Captain replied through clenched teeth. 'If the scoundrel sold his secret to the Cat Fish or had the truth tortured out of him, they'd know our every move.'

Whisker laboured to his feet. The map was still *his* responsibility.

'We can chase – them down –' he gasped. 'We can get –' His head spun. He felt himself swaying and collapsed into Horace.

'You're not going anywhere,' the Captain said firmly. A cheese-knife-blow to the head requires rest and recuperation.'

Whisker looked at Ruby for support.

'The important thing is that you're alive,' she said, giving him a hard stare. 'The key and the map are long g ...'

'Don't give me that rubbish,' Whisker shouted. 'We haven't come this far just to give up!' He pushed Horace aside and drew his sword. 'Tell me which way they went.'

Expressionless, Ruby pointed down the mountain.

The Captain took a deep breath and sighed. 'What *have* you been teaching him, Ruby?'

'Stubbornness, for a start,' Horace muttered.

'That's not stubbornness,' Ruby said with a hint of admiration, 'that's determination.'

Without a response, Whisker staggered into the trees. He knew it was more than determination – it was *desperation*.

He found Eaton sitting on the top step, staring silently at the ground. Whisker felt a sudden rush of pity for the young mouse.

Poor little fellow, he thought. *He's just a kid. How many school boys face chameleons, death drops and Cat Fish all in one day?*

Eaton looked up.

'D-don't go,' he pleaded. 'T-they'll kill you.'

'I have to,' Whisker answered. '… I just have to.'

'But why?' Eaton asked.

Whisker had never revealed his true reason for wanting the map. He knew it was nothing more than a childish hope. But Eaton *was* a child and he deserved an answer. Whisker knelt down beside him.

'You have a sister, Eaton,' he said. 'And I know you want to see her again.'

Eaton nodded.

'I have a sister too,' Whisker explained. 'Her name is Anna. She's only little, but she loves books nearly as much as you do, though she only looks at the pictures. I used to read her stories about gallant heroes on dangerous adventures. Her favourite story was *The Brave Little Mouse and the Twelve Tigers.*'

'I know that one,' Eaton said.

'Then you'll know what the mouse did to save his family from the tigers,' Whisker said. 'Twelve tigers are six times worse than a couple of Cat Fish!'

Eaton managed a reserved smile.

'Without the map,' Whisker continued, 'I may never see my sister again. What kind of ending would that be?'

'A miserable one,' Eaton answered, rising to his feet. 'You'd better hurry if you want to catch them. Cats are nearly as quick as tigers!'

Whisker half leapt, half fell down the rough stone steps with Eaton scampering behind him.

What a brave little mouse, Whisker thought to himself.

'Wait for us!' Horace cried, bursting from the jungle with the rest of the crew. 'We're coming too! ... one thousand two hundred and sixty three ... one thousand two hundred and sixty two ...'

The Pie Rats reached the bottom of the stairs and continued along the main track, only stopping to catch their breaths once they heard the roar of Silver Falls.

The Captain pointed to fresh paw prints in the mud.

'The Cat Fish took the river track,' he panted. 'I suspect the *Silver Sardine* is anchored in the estuary. We have two options – follow their trail, or take the shortcut back to the *Apple Pie* and hope Fred has baked enough pies for an improvised sea assault.'

'*Shortcut?*' Ruby muttered. 'I'd hardly call marmosets, mudskippers and sinking sand a time saver.'

Seven heads nodded their agreement and the Pie Rats raced towards the river. Whisker's head still ached. He was hungry, tired and thirsty, but the adrenalin pumping through his body kept his legs moving. Deep down inside he knew they would never catch their enemies on foot unless Prowler and Cleopatra stopped for a catnap – rats and mice simply didn't have the speed.

The overgrown track continued along the muddy bank of the river. Drawing level with a patch of waterweed, Whisker stopped and stared into the rushing water. The rapids were smaller than at the foot of the falls, but the current still moved at a tremendous pace.

He picked up a stick and hurled it into the river. In moments, it had been swept away.

'Wait!' he shouted.

The Pie Rats skidded to a halt.

'What have you seen?' the Captain cried, drawing his sword.

'Speed!' Whisker replied.

'Huh?' Horace said, puzzled.

'The river!' Whisker exclaimed. 'Look how fast it's moving. And there are logs and vines all over the ground.'

'Everything we need to build a raft!' the Captain applauded.

'Everything *except* life vests,' Mr Tribble added under his breath.

'Lighten up, Tribble,' Horace said, grabbing the closest log. 'We won't let you drown – not when you're carrying a backpack of silver!'

Mr Tribble didn't look impressed.

'Here, make yourself useful,' Ruby said, throwing him the ball of string. 'A tight knot is a safe knot.'

The rats rolled half-a-dozen small logs over to the riverbank while the mice tied them together with Ruby's string. Smudge pointed his tiny arms this way and that, trying to direct traffic, but generally got in everyone's way.

When the sixth log was secured, the raft was pushed into the shallows and the crew clambered aboard. The Captain stood at the back of the raft with a long stick in his paws and a loop of string tied around his waist. The rest of the crew crouched on their knees and held onto small cords of string.

'Keep an eye on the river, Smudge,' the Captain ordered as he pushed off from the bank, 'and tell us if you see any white water rapids!'

Mr Tribble gulped and gripped tighter on the string. Horace tapped a log with his hook and grinned. 'Safe as a mouse's house!'

The raft bobbed and bumped its way into the centre of the river, gathering speed. Once the river took control there was nothing the Captain could do. The vessel travelled four times faster than the Pie Rats could ever run, making up ground with every splash.

Small rapids approached. The front of the raft dipped under the water, splashing cool water in the faces of the Pie Rats. The raft creaked, the string strained and the logs scraped over shallow rocks, but the vessel held together.

Whisker felt invigorated and full of hope. His tail dangled over the side of the raft, soaking up the energy of the river. Wide-eyed, he scanned the riverbank for any signs of the Cat Fish.

We're getting closer, he thought. *I can feel it.*

The small vessel turned a sharp bend in the river where the water was deep and wide. Smudge flew frantically above the crew, looping-the-loop to grab the Captain's attention.

'What is it?' the Captain asked, peering into the jungle.

Smudge pointed to the river. The water moved swiftly, but there were no signs of raging rapids, whirlpools or protruding logs.

Whisker felt a sudden stabbing pain at the end of his tail. Instinctively, he whipped it out of the water and yelped. Looking down, he saw a circle of tiny teeth marks in his skin.

Horrified, the rest of the Pie Rats grabbed their own tails and shuffled closer to the centre of the raft. Grey and red shapes appeared in the water beside them, circling the vessel. Fins beat the surface of the river, tails splashed wildly about. Peering overboard, Whisker caught glimpses of silvery, red-flecked eyes.

'Red-bellied piranhas!' Mr Tribble exclaimed. 'They're in a feeding frenzy. One taste of flesh and they're hooked!'

Whisker's tail froze in fear.

'Keep low,' the Captain ordered. 'The raft is our protection.'

The splashes grew louder as more piranhas joined the school of attacking fish. Amid the chaos, a strange, scratching noise echoed through the logs. Whisker felt his left leg creeping away from his body.

'THE LOG!' Horace shouted. 'It's moving!'

Startled, Whisker looked down to see water between his legs. The piranhas had chewed through the string and one of the logs was drifting away from the raft – the log Whisker and Horace were kneeling on.

Ruby grabbed a candy cane from her backpack and hooked it around the wood, attempting to drag the log closer. Whisker glimpsed the snapping teeth of piranhas beneath him and tried desperately to keep his balance. Horace howled in terror as his legs ran out of stretch.

Steadying himself, Whisker grabbed Horace by the scruff of his neck and leapt from the log onto the centre of the raft. The candy cane slipped and Ruby toppled backwards into Eaton, still clutching the stump of the cane in her paws – its end gnawed clean off.

The raft began to wobble.

'They're eating through the rest of the string!' Mr

Tribble gasped.

'Hold on!' the Captain roared. 'I'll try to steer us to shore.'

He stood up and thrust his stick into the water. It shuddered violently. Gasping, he pulled it out again, half the length it had been.

'Ratbeard be kind!' he exclaimed. 'They'll eat anything!'

The Pie Rats struggled to hold the raft together as, one by one, the logs began separating. Smudge tried to grab the crew's attention, but the Captain brushed him aside with his paw.

The raft reached another bend in the river and white water rapids approached.

'We're done for!' Mr Tribble shouted.

Whisker looked ahead. The rapids extended a short way and then suddenly disappeared – the whole river seemed to disappear into the distant horizon.

It's not possible, Whisker thought.

Smudge dive-bombed the raft and suddenly it clicked.

Of course, Whisker thought. *The river isn't disappearing. It's a ...*

'WATERFALL!' Ruby shouted.

The Pie Rats braced themselves for the impact as the pile of logs that had once resembled a raft plummeted over the edge of the falls.

Whisker let go of the string and leapt for his life. Beneath him, the waterfall cascaded into a wide, sandy pool. He dived towards the sparkling water with outstretched arms, hoping the pool was as deep as it was wide.

Slicing through the water like a pin, he descended to the icy depths with no sunken logs or submerged rocks in his path. Aware of the danger he still faced, he spun his body around and kicked his way to the surface.

Gasping for air, he burst from the pool and waited for the piranhas to attack. Nothing happened. No vicious bites. No painful nibbles. He tasted the water. It wasn't sweet like the mountain river – it was salty, like the sea.

The river estuary, he thought.

He looked around. In the centre of the pool, Eaton hung off a log, while Ruby straightened her crimson eye patch. The Captain swam after his hat and Horace splashed in the shallows, laughing at his good fortune. Whisker couldn't relax – there were still two Cat Fish to catch.

He paddled over to the shore and staggered onto the sand. Bathed in the afternoon sunlight, the fine grains felt warm beneath his toes. Barely a breeze blew from the ocean.

Nearby, Mr Tribble stood like a statue, staring out to sea. Whisker followed his gaze, over the pool, beyond the estuary and past the breaking waves of the shoreline to a single silver ship.

His heart sank. The *Silver Sardine* was right in front of him, but it was already sailing away. Helplessly, Whisker watched as the ship rounded an island to the north and disappeared from sight. He was too late. The key and the map were gone.

The rest of the crew dragged themselves from the pool, silently gathering around Whisker. Talk seemed pointless – even for Horace.

'Smudge is sending word to the *Apple Pie*,' the Captain said, finally breaking the silence. 'It's too dangerous for us to cross the mudflat again. We'll meet the ship on the southern shore of the estuary. I suggest we get moving.'

'How do we know the *Apple Pie* is still hidden?' Mr

Tribble asked with concern.

'We don't,' the Captain replied. 'But no smoke is always a good sign.'

Whisker sat hunched over in the back of the rowboat. It was night and his sombre mood hadn't changed. He was tired, sore, and utterly miserable.

Fish Eye Fred rowed the companions through the surf to where the *Apple Pie* waited beyond the breakers. Emmie, in her usual cheery state, was overjoyed to see the companions alive. She threw her arms around her brother and hugged him tightly. Whisker had never seen so much relief on Eaton's face.

Pete was predictably annoyed to hear of their misadventure and even more annoyed to discover that no one had thought to make a copy of the map. A stern look from the Captain ensured he kept his sarcastic remarks to himself.

Fred wasted no time in offering a welcome supper to the hungry crew.

'Berry pies, apple pies or potato pies?' he asked.

'All of the above,' Horace drooled.

Fred laid a selection of fresh pies in the centre of the navigation room. In minutes, the pies were no more than a pile of crumbs. Fred trudged off to get dessert – a second round of pies, while Pete sat muttering to himself in the corner.

'If it's any consolation, Quartermaster Pete,' Mr Tribble said politely, 'I have the two herbs you requested – though, they may be a little soggy.'

Pete screwed up his nose. 'Equal quantities of each?'

'Of course,' Mr Tribble replied. 'Incidentally, which herb is for sleeping?'

'The roots are for sleeping,' Pete stated. 'The eyeballs give you energy.' He frowned at Horace. 'I thought I made that clear.'

'Err ... look what else we've got,' Horace said, changing the subject. 'A silver dinner set.' He began pulling knives, forks and plates from his backpack. 'They'll need some polishing but ...'

'I'll take care of that, Uncle Horace,' Emmie said, snatching a plate from him. 'I'm the new *Hygiene Officer*, you know.'

'Really?' Horace said, glancing at Pete.

'She wanted a title,' Pete sniffled, 'and she likes cleaning. You should see the galley. It's spotless.'

'Come on, Eaton!' Emmie said, grabbing her brother by the sleeve. 'You're going to help me polish these plates while you tell me all about the island.'

'Yes, sis,' Eaton reluctantly agreed.

The Pie Rats removed the remaining silverware from their backpacks and laid them on the floor. Whisker had no backpack – the Cat Fish had torn it to shreds. He slipped unnoticed through the doorway and wandered across the deck.

It was late in the evening, but the moon had not yet risen. The ocean was dead calm, not a breath of wind stirred. Whisker felt like he was drifting on a dark sea of despair. He peered up at the stars and searched for some comfort.

My family are watching these same stars, he told himself – *if they're awake ... if they're even alive.*

He heard the sound of the Pie Rats muttering inside and felt a surge of anger rise in his chest.

They've forgotten about the key already, he thought spitefully. *They have their treasure. It's all they care about.*

Smudge landed gently on the bulwark next to him. At the sight of the small, inquisitive creature, Whisker's anger quickly drained away.

'Hello, Smudge,' he said wearily. 'Don't like silver either?'

Smudge shook his head and pointed to Whisker's anchor pendant.

'You like gold,' Whisker said.

Smudge shook his head again.

'Anchors?' Whisker said confused.

Smudge shook his head a third time.

'*Hope*?' Whisker guessed. 'An anchor is the symbol of hope.'

Smudge nodded.

Whisker ran his finger over his pendant and sighed. 'I once had hope. Now I have nothing … not even a stupid plan.'

Smudge pointed to the mainsail and flapped two arms like a bird.

Whisker looked up. The sail hung limply from the mast.

'A sail's no good without wind, Smudge, even if it is our precious eagle. Besides, the Cat Fish could be halfway to the Island of Destiny by now.'

Smudge didn't respond. The rat and the fly stared into the darkness. There was silence.

Whisker felt the light touch of a paw on his shoulder but heard no one. He didn't looking around – only one rat was that quiet.

'How long have you been here, *Ruby*?' he asked.

214

Ruby lowered her paw and placed it on the carved edge of the ship.

'Long enough to know you don't want silver for your birthday,' she replied. 'I can't blame you. That stuff reeks of monkeys.'

Whisker tried to smile but inwardly he felt even worse. He'd just written-off Ruby as a treasure-hungry silver-lover, and judging by the shuffling footsteps behind her, he'd made the same mistake with Horace.

'What have I missed?' Horace asked. 'Have you come up with a cunning plan to get the key back?'

'I've got nothing,' Whisker mumbled.

'Oh well,' Horace shrugged. 'You'll think of something … you always do.'

Not this time, Whisker thought miserably.

Three rats and a blowfly stared into the darkness, lost in their own thoughts. The stillness of the ocean was much too quiet for Horace.

'The moon's coming up,' he said, pointing to the east with his hook. 'I can see the glow … Yes, there it is. Look how fast it's moving.'

Whisker watched the crescent moon rise majestically over the horizon. It cleared the edge of the ocean and then suddenly disappeared.

'Hey!' Horace exclaimed. 'Where did it go?'

Whisker studied the sky. There wasn't a single cloud in sight, but the moon was definitely blocked by something.

It only took him a moment to figure it out. He'd seen the shape once before on a moonlit night and its shimmering outline gave it away. The *Silver Sardine* wasn't half an ocean away. It was drifting right in front of him.

TWENTY

Rat Burglars

The Captain held a telescope to his eye and peered into the blackness. The crew stood beside him, swords drawn, ready for action.

'No sign of movement on the *Sardine*,' he whispered, 'I think we've caught them napping – though it's too dark to be certain.' He lowered the telescope. 'An aerial sweep of the ship will give us a clearer picture – Smudge?'

Smudge nodded his head and, with a faint buzz of wings, flew across the glassy ocean to explore. The Pie Rats awaited his return.

'It was a stroke of good luck you spotted them,' the Captain said quietly to Horace. 'It's even more fortunate the wind, or lack of it, prevented their escape.'

'Right place, right time …' Horace muttered, giving Whisker a wink.

Whisker smiled. Hope was back.

'What's the battle plan, Uncle,' Ruby asked. 'Stealth-attack or single-rat-infiltration?'

'I'm not sending you in alone, if that's what you're asking,' the Captain replied firmly. 'You may be quiet, but it if comes to a fight with six cats, you'll need backup.'

'I'll take Whisker,' Ruby replied without hesitation. 'He

needs to pass his *Swords-rat-ship* test sooner or later.'

Whisker wasn't sure if he should feel proud or downright terrified.

'Are you sure he's ready?' the Captain asked warily. 'I have no doubts about his commitment, but *one* lesson …?'

'He's ready,' Ruby said firmly. 'His reaction speed on the cliff top was quicker than any apprentice I've seen.'

She gave Whisker a look of admiration. Whisker straightened his back and tried not to blush.

'And he's got a secret weapon,' Horace added, 'his tail!'

'Very well,' the Captain agreed. 'Whisker can join Ruby, Smudge and myself …'

'And me!' Horace cut in.

'And Horace …' the Captain added.

'Don't forget me,' Fred said.

The Captain sighed. 'Whisker can join Ruby, Smudge, Horace, Fred, yours truly, and anyone else who's crazy enough to sign up for a suicidal stealth mission to retrieve the map and key –' He took a deep breath.

'I'll guard the rowboat,' Pete said dryly. 'My pencil leg is hardly an item of *stealth*.'

The mice were in no hurry to volunteer for anything cat-related and the Captain assigned them duties on the *Apple Pie*. Smudge soon returned with the news they all wanted to hear: the Cat Fish were fast asleep.

'Prowler is dozing in the crow's-nest,' the Captain relayed, 'and Master Meow is draped over the wheel. The others must be asleep in their cabins –' He hesitated and looked directly at Pete. 'Incidentally, there was no sign of Rat Bait onboard.'

'That proves nothing!' Pete snapped. 'Nothing at all!'

Avoiding a bitter argument, the Captain moved on.

'Gather your swords and meet me in the rowboat. We leave in two minutes.'

One and a half minutes later, Whisker climbed down the rope ladder to the small rowboat. Ruby, Pete and the Captain were already seated, anxiously waiting to depart. Fred was only a few rungs behind Whisker. The boat rocked from side to side as the giant clambered aboard and took his place at the oars.

'Where's that good-for-nothing Horace?' Pete sniffled. 'It will be daylight before the lazy lout turns up.'

'Here I am!' Horace exclaimed from the top of the ladder. 'I had a few *survival* items to gather.'

As Horace scurried down the rope, Whisker noticed he was wearing a backpack – an extremely *full* backpack. Whisker shot him a look of concern.

'Every mission needs a Plan B,' Horace whispered, taking the seat next to Whisker.

'Shh,' Pete hissed.

Horace shut his mouth and the small vessel began slicing through the still water.

The crescent moon hung directly above the *Silver Sardine*, guiding the thieves to their prize. A faint breeze blew gently from the east, but only the soft splashes of Fred's oars penetrated the night air. Smudge flew ahead as a precaution, on the off chance that the Cat Fish had woken for a midnight snack.

Silently, the rowboat pulled alongside the armour-plated hull and Fred stowed the oars. Hundreds of crumpled sardine tins lined the sides of the ship, providing protection – as well as convenient paw holds.

Smudge peered down from the deck and gestured with four arms.

'All clear,' the Captain whispered. 'Let's go.'

One by one, the Pie Rats scaled the metallic hull, grabbing hold of rivets and the edges of tins. Pete remained in the rowboat with his sword drawn.

The deck of the *Silver Sardine* was a pigsty of fish bones, half-eaten biscuits and empty milk bottles. The Cat Fish had clearly been celebrating their successful acquisition. Master Meow, the silver tabby, slept standing up with his arms draped over the ship's wheel and his head dangling forward. His glass eye gleamed in the moonlight. The tip of Prowler's blue-grey tail could be seen hanging over the side of the crow's-nest.

On the Captain's command, the Pie Rats tiptoed towards the staircase in the centre of the deck. Clumsily, Horace kicked a milk bottle with his foot. With a loud *TING, RATTLE, RATTLE* it rolled across the deck.

The Pie Rats froze.

The bottle bumped over a biscuit and came to a stop in a pile of fish heads. All eyes fixed on the sleeping cats. Master Meow didn't stir. Prowler's tail remained motionless.

Ruby glared at Horace, silently fuming. Horace mouthed *whoops* and the Pie Rats continued their cautious advance.

Closer to the stairs, the Captain gestured to Fred and pointed to the navigation room. Fred nodded in understanding and headed for the doorway. Smudge flew to the top of a mast to keep an eye on the deck, and the four remaining rats descended the narrow staircase to the cabins below.

A lantern hung from a wall at the bottom of the first flight of stairs, spreading a faint glow through the main corridor. The whole place smelt like rotten fish. Whisker resisted the urge to hold his nose.

You're a warrior now, he tried to convince himself. *Warriors don't hold their noses. They hold their swords.*

He touched the handle of his scissor sword, hanging by his side, and pictured himself wielding it in battle. He didn't want to disappoint Ruby but he still had his doubts about his ability. Cat Fish fought with cheese knives – not sticks.

Trying to remain positive, Whisker refocused on his surrounds. Four doorways lined the tight corridor. A loud wheezing sound drifted through the first doorway to the right – the door was ajar.

The Captain looked straight at Horace and motioned to the door. Horace slipped through the gap and disappeared into the darkness.

The second door was painted bright red and stood closed. Two words were scratched into its shiny surface: *Girls Only.*

Cleopatra and Siamese Sally, Whisker thought. He'd run into them once before in a dark corridor, and on that occasion he'd only just survived. He felt his tail begin to shake.

Ruby pointed to the writing on the door and flashed Whisker a mischievous grin. She slowly turned the handle and stepped inside.

There were two doorways left. A heavy oak door stood at the end of the corridor, decorated with an intricately carved fish skeleton. It was undoubtedly the Captain's cabin. Opposite the ladies' cabin was a partially open doorway. A terrible fishy smell wafted through the gap.

As the Captain crept towards Sabre's cabin, Whisker knew his fate. Grabbing his nose, he entered the pungent smelling mess room of the Cat Fish.

The mess room was a *mess*. A huge table stood in the centre of the cramped space, covered with the remains of a seafood feast. Fish heads, octopus tentacles, mussel shells and sardine tails sprawled onto the floor. Unwashed milk bottles were stacked against the wall to form crude towers, waiting to topple over at the slightest touch.

Whisker climbed onto a stool and peered down at the clutter on the table. He caught a glimpse of a silver plate buried deep beneath the scraps and wondered what other precious items lay concealed in the heap.

Surely the map isn't under there, he thought.

He glanced around the room, searching for clues. Light streamed through a gap under a closed door in the far corner.

The ship's galley, he told himself. *More fishy food!*

Carefully, Whisker climbed down from the stool and navigated his way past an eel's tail and three sea cucumbers, towards the small door. Refusing to release his nose, he turned the handle with his free paw. The door unlatched with a soft *click* and opened inwards.

Whisker wasn't prepared for what he saw. A single lantern hung from a rafter, illuminating the small room. The floor was littered with empty milk bottles and sardine skeletons. In the centre of the room, sleeping soundly on a kitchen bench was the unmistakable striped and spotted body of Captain Sabre. Partly covered by his left paw, lay an open map and a three-toothed key.

Whisker stared at Sabre, not daring to blink. He half expected the vicious captain to wake up at any moment and fly at him in a terrible rage. The last time Whisker had been this close to Sabre, he had thrown a mug of Apple Fizz in his face. He doubted Sabre was one to forgive or forget.

With a silent breath, Whisker stepped closer.

This is what you wanted, he told himself. *There's no backing down.*

He removed his paw from his nose and the unsavoury smell of Sabre's fish-shake breath filled his nostrils. Trying to ignore Sabre's purring snores, he reached out and touched the key. It was smooth and clean. He could see the words, *Rock of Hope* written on the oval handle. Painted rocks and the outline of a mountain decorated the shaft of the key, and a small X lay in the centre of the lower tooth.

This is the King's Key, Whisker marvelled.

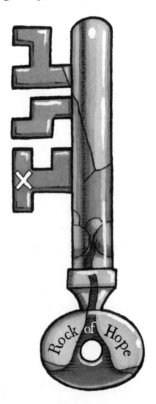

Ever so gently, he lifted Sabre's paw and slid the key towards him.

Sabre stirred.

Petrified, Whisker stopped, still clutching Sabre's paw, not daring to move.

Sabre burped, sighed and continued sleeping.

Whisker tried again. Delicately, he slid the key from the bench and slipped in into his pocket.

Nearly there.

He moved his fingers back to the bench, gripped the crumpled edge of the map and gave it a soft tug. The map slid freely over the wooden surface and over the side of the bench. With utmost care, Whisker lowered Sabre's paw gently back down.

... like stealing milk from a kitten, he thought proudly.

He shuffled his way around scattered milk bottles, folding the map as he went. Trying to contain his excitement, he stuffed the map into his pocket and stepped through the open doorway, into the mess room.

A loud shout echoed from the corridor beyond. 'FIERY FURNACES! THERE'S A PARASITE IN MY HAMMOCK!'

Sabre's eyes shot open. Whisker's heart skipped a beat.

The furious Captain took one look at the empty bench and leapt to his feet.

'You little thief!' he snarled, grabbing a cheese knife from a shelf.

Terrified, Whisker spun on his heel and ran. Halfway across the mess room, he felt the squishy shape of a sea cucumber under his left foot and slipped backwards, hitting the floor with a violent *THUD*. He looked up to see Sabre standing over him, his hazel eyes ablaze with rage.

Captain Sabre

Before Whisker could react, Sabre swung his razor-sharp weapon above his head and prepared to strike.

THUMP!

The tip of Sabre's cheese knife sliced into a wooden rafter and held fast. Sabre heaved with all his might but the blade wouldn't budge.

Whisker was familiar with the saying, *not enough room to swing a cat.* Tonight it was a case of *not enough room for a cat to swing.*

By the time Sabre had pulled his knife from the rafter, Whisker had thrown his body under the table.

There was a sickening *CRACK* above him as the table split in two, cleaved by Sabre's sharp blade. Fish eyes and squid ink rained down.

Whisker leapt clear of the seafood deluge and collided with a tower of milk bottles. He covered his head as the bottles bounced over him, rattling and rolling across the floor in all directions.

Sabre heaved the broken table out of the way and skulked towards him.

The muffled shouts of Ruby rang out from the corridor, but with a sideways step, Sabre blocked Whisker's escape route.

Mustering all of his strength, Whisker pulled himself to his feet and drew his sword.

Plough Guard, he told himself, preparing to engage.

Sabre stopped in his tracks and roared with laughter.

'… Well, well, well! The *little captain* has found himself a sword. It's a pity you'll only get to use it once …'

'I've defeated heaps of enemies!' Whisker lied. 'Now step aside.'

'Oooh!' Sabre taunted. 'Is that any way to speak to

your gracious host? Why don't you calm down and the two of us can have a little drink together like civilised gentlemen.'

Sabre picked up a full milk bottle and hurled it at Whisker.

Whisker ducked. The bottle smashed into a tower of empty bottles, spraying milky shards of glass all over the floor. Whisker looked up to see a second bottle flying in his direction.

Strike of Wrath, he thought, just in time to slice the bottle in half.

A third bottle raced towards him.

Crooked Strike – tail manoeuvre. This time Whisker caught the bottle with his tail.

'Two can play at this,' he hissed, flicking the bottle at Sabre.

Sabre deflected the bottle with his cheese knife and charged at Whisker with a vicious snarl.

Study your surrounds, Whisker recalled, sweeping his eyes across the floor. He took a quick step to his left and raised his sword in an Ox Guard position.

Sabre was almost within striking range when he suddenly howled in pain and stumbled backwards, hopping on one foot. He pulled a large chunk of glass from his heel and tried to steady himself.

The door to the corridor swung open, and Ruby came into view, driving Cleopatra and Sally down the narrow passage.

'Get out!' she shouted.

Whisker knew this was his only chance to escape. It was now or never.

Control the flow of the fight, he told himself.

He looked at Sabre, shifted his eyes to the door and immediately he knew what to do. Lowering his sword in a Fool's Guard position, he leapt over the line of broken glass and stormed towards Sabre.

With his defences down, Whisker was an easy target. Sabre lowered his injured foot to the ground and swung his blade through the air in a wide arc.

Whisker was ready. His sword shot upwards, colliding with Sabre's cheese knife, and sent the weapon flying off course. Then, using the impact of the blow, he propelled his body downwards. Before Sabre knew what was happening, Whisker had disappeared between his legs and was sliding out the door in a pile of slippery sea scallops.

'Mission accomplished!' Whisker cried, skidding to a halt in the centre of the corridor.

'Let's go!' Ruby shouted, pulling him to his feet. 'The Captain's on the deck.'

They darted up the corridor with Sally and Cleopatra hot on their heels. Horace burst from a doorway, spilling sticks of explosives from his open backpack.

Furious Fur, tangled in a hammock, staggered blindly after him and collided with Cleopatra and Sally. The three cats fell to the floor in a hissing ball of twine and fur. A moment later, Sabre, unable to stop, sprawled on top of them.

Horace wrenched the lantern from the wall and stuck three fuses in the flame. They instantly sparked to life. He dropped the hissing sticks at the bottom of the stairs and sprinted up with Ruby and Whisker. The cats took one look at the explosives and leapt through the nearest doorway.

'ARE YOU INSANE, HORACE?' Ruby shouted. 'YOU'LL KILL US ALL!'

Horace was too busy ripping off his backpack to respond.

Whisker saw a brightly coloured stick tumble out and roll down the stairs. It had four fins and a pointy top.

'Fireworks!' he exclaimed. 'Genius!'

'Shh,' Horace hissed. 'You'll spoil the surprise!'

The three rats reached the top of the stairs to find Fred and the Captain battling Prowler and Master Meow. Smudge buzzed around Meow's head, poking the enraged cat in his one good eye.

Horace threw his backpack on the deck and smashed the lantern on top of it. With a symphony of sparks, the flames ignited the fuses.

Master Meow and Prowler screeched in terror and sprinted into the navigation room, slamming the door behind them.

'Time to go!' the Captain shouted.

The Pie Rats scurried over the side of the ship and tumbled into the rowboat.

BANG! WIZZ! HISS! CRACKLE!

The *Silver Sardine* lit up like a psychedelic Christmas tree.

'Oh my precious paws!' Pete gasped. 'What the flaming rat's tail is going on?'

'Happy half-graduation, Whisker!' Horace cried, falling into the bottom of the boat.

'Get us out of here, Fred!' the Captain bellowed. 'NOW!'

Fred rowed, Pete cursed and the fireworks exploded in a dazzling display of colour and sound. Rockets raced high. Sparks rained down. Red, gold and green flashes filled the sky – every colour majestically reflected in the silver hull of the ship.

'I haven't seen a performance this good since the Gourmet Gunpowder incident!' Horace laughed.

Pete looked far from impressed.

'I take it one of you has the map and key,' he sniffled.

'Ask *Fish Boy*,' Ruby grinned, pointing to a half eaten sardine hanging from Whisker's belt.

'Ooogh!' Horace winced. 'That explains the awful smell!'

Whisker threw the sardine overboard and tried to hide his embarrassment.

'E-e-everything's in my pockets,' he stammered.

'An easy grab-and-run, was it?' Pete said sceptically.

'Not exactly …' Whisker began.

'Sabre thought he'd add Whisker to his clam chowder,' Ruby chimed in. He didn't count on Whisker's *Fool's Guard-Horace Shuffle* combo.'

'Way to go, Whisker!' Horace applauded. 'I said it was a stellar move!'

'Congratulations, Whisker,' the Captain said proudly. 'You've just passed your third apprenticeship test, paws down. Sabre is no easy cat to …'

'Err, Captain,' Pete interrupted. 'I'm sorry to rain on Whisker's parade, but I'm certain those lights weren't there a minute ago.'

'W-what lights?' Horace spluttered.

'The lantern lights moving towards the floating inferno, you half-brained hamster!' Pete snapped.

Whisker peered into the distance. Pete was right. Several groups of lanterns approached from the east, moving swiftly in the strengthening breeze.

'Someone's seen our little pyrotechnics display,' the

Captain observed, his voice suddenly grave. 'Can you identify them, Fred?'

Fred swivelled his enormous eye in the direction of the lanterns.

'Three ships,' he grunted. 'Two *Claws-of-War* and a *Dreadnaught* ...'

'Rotten pies to *Dreadnaughts*!' Horace muttered. 'There goes our easy escape!'

TWENTY-ONE

A Not-so-easy Escape

'The game's up,' Pete groaned. 'We're sitting dodos in a rowboat to extinction!'

'Hold your tongue,' the Captain hissed. 'I doubt Thunderclaw's seen us through all the sparks and the smoke. If we can reach the *Apple Pie* before the fireworks stop, we may have a chance to escape unseen.'

Pete jabbed Fred with his pencil. 'Row faster, you big oaf! But do it quietly.'

Fred took no notice of Pete's demands and continued his slow and steady strokes. The rest of the crew remained silent, staring back at the chaotic scene, hoping darkness would conceal their escape.

Soon only the occasional stray rocket exploded from the *Silver Sardine*, a clear sign the performance was drawing to a close.

The black shape of the *Apple Pie* came into view and the Captain issued a hasty command: 'Fly ahead, Smudge. Prepare the mice for an immediate launch the moment we're on deck.'

Smudge gave the Captain a two-armed salute and buzzed into the darkness.

'What's our destination?' Horace asked anxiously.

The Captain considered his options. 'We can't sail east with a headwind and three warships in the way, and seeing as we're still close to the Island of Kings …'

'Don't even think about it!' Pete broke in. 'No one goes in *there*.'

'Shush, you!' Horace scolded. 'It's the quickest route to the Island of Destiny and no one's crazy enough to follow us through.'

'Follow us through what?' Whisker asked in confusion.

Pete screwed up his nose. 'The *passage*, of course. 'The passage past Devil's Cliffs.'

Whisker looked horrified. 'But don't the devils throw …'

'Old wives' tales,' Horace cut in. 'We're more likely to run aground on a submerged rock.'

'And *then* have an avalanche of stones hurled at us,' Pete muttered.

Horace brushed the comment aside with a dismissive wave of his hook. 'Relax, they won't even see us coming – it's the middle of the night.'

Pete stamped his pencil leg on the bottom of the boat. 'Tasmanian devils are *nocturnal,* you uneducated eggplant!'

The Captain ignored the argument and called for a vote.

'Better the devils you know,' Ruby said, raising her paw.

Horace stuck his hook straight in the air. Fred added his support with an affirmative grunt. As an apprentice, Whisker didn't have a vote, so he kept his paws by his side and waited for the outcome.

'It's decided,' the Captain said, raising his paw to Pete's dismay. 'We sail through the passage.'

The *Apple Pie* slipped silently away from the midnight commotion. The fireworks display had ended, but the party was just beginning.

The wind carried the frantic sounds of the Cat Fish across the water. Whisker heard hisses and shouts as the frenzied felines scurried across the deck, preparing to flee or fight.

The warships had not yet fired their cannons. Presumably, a fireworks-exploding pirate ship required careful investigation before an appropriate course of action was taken. The Pie Rats had no desire to find out. In minutes, the *Apple Pie* was beyond earshot and sailing through the mouth of the perilous passage.

The moon provided sufficient light for the Pie Rats to see where they were going. No lanterns burned, no voices spoke. The black cliffs of Phoenix Island rose ominously to the north, blocking the stars. The shallow water of the mangrove swamp lay to the south. The Captain set a course through the centre of the passage, where the water was deepest.

It wasn't long before the mangroves disappeared and the towering southern cliffs took their place. The passage curved north-west and the cliffs closed in on both sides. A fierce wind howled through the narrow gap, driving the *Apple Pie* further into the dark abyss. There was no thought of using the eagle sail. The devils would undoubtedly spot the golden shape the moment it rose above the cliffs.

Dawn approached and the passage veered west. Whisker had spent much of the journey hanging off the foremast, without spotting a single devil, and he was growing more anxious by the minute. The faint glow of the dawn sky came as no relief. He knew that with every orange-rimmed cloud came the danger of discovery. Light was the Pie Rat's new enemy.

The open sea grew visible at the western end of the passage as the first rays of the morning sun struck the tops of the cliffs. For a moment, Whisker thought they were going to make it. He scrambled higher up the rigging for a clearer vantage point. What he saw made his tail shiver in terror.

Lining the ridge of the northern cliff was an army of shaggy black beasts. Their ears were red with anger. Their mouths were open and snarling. Their sharp claws slashed through the air in a warlike display of rage.

Panic-stricken, Whisker watched the creatures pick up jagged rocks and drag them to the edge of the cliff.

'D-D-DEVILS!' he shouted. 'STARBOARD SIDE!'

The crew gasped in startled horror as the first wave of projectiles splashed into the water, narrowly missing the bow of the ship. The Captain spun the wheel hard left and the *Apple Pie* lurched to its port side.

'Watch out for the rocks!' Pete screeched.

'I'm watching!' the Captain shouted, fixing his eyes on the cliff top.

'Not those rocks!' Pete hollered. 'The rocks we're about to collide with!'

Whisker looked down. Dark shapes rose from the surface of the indigo water, blocking half the passage.

The Captain jerked the *Apple Pie* to its starboard side, barely clearing the rocks but forcing the ship dangerously close to Devil's Cliffs.

'Shipwrecks ... sandbars ... warships ... rocks ...' Horace groaned. 'There's always something in the way!'

The second wave of missiles rained down. This time a handful of rocks hit their target, smashing craterlike holes in the deck and splintering the side of the bulwark. The devils threw their paws in the air and hooted in delight.

'We can't sustain this for long, Captain!' Pete shouted. 'Once they puncture the hull, we're history!'

'Return fire!' Ruby hissed. 'Are the cannons ready?'

'The angle's too steep,' Horace cried. 'We need a catapult!'

'There's no time to build one,' Mr Tribble called from the navigation room. 'Let's hope the devils retreat with the daylight.'

'Fat chance!' Pete shot back. 'They're devils, not vampires!'

Whisker knew Pete was right – but Mr Tribble wasn't necessarily *wrong* … The *Apple Pie* lay in the shadows of the cliffs, but the tips of the cutlery masts were bathed in sunlight. Rays of light bounced off the shiny prongs of the giant fork.

'Emmie! Eaton!' Whisker shouted. 'Have you finished polishing the plates?'

'Almost …' Emmie squeaked.

'I need them NOW!' Whisker yelled.

Whisker heard the clatter of silverware from the navigation room, followed by the crash of rocks hitting the deck. A rock whizzed past his head, tearing a hole in the sail.

'Hurry!' he shouted.

Emmie and Eaton appeared at the doorway with two piles of silver dishes.

'Bring me the shiniest plates!' Whisker barked.

Ruby and Horace leapt over the holes in the deck to reach the two mice. They hastily grabbed three plates each and dashed towards the mast.

A dozen rocks hurtled down.

'EARS UP!' Whisker shouted.

Ruby jumped back as a large rock hit the side of the hull, bursting through the wood with a splintering *CRACK!* It was immediately followed by the sound of rushing water.

'We've sprung a leak!' Pete shouted from the stairwell.

'Plug it with a pie!' the Captain bellowed.

Fred ran below deck to help Pete while Horace and Ruby scampered up the mast with the plates. They quickly reached Whisker at the top of the mast, his torso bathed in golden sunlight.

'Two plates each,' he directed, taking a plate in each paw. 'Use them like mirrors. Aim the sunlight directly at the devils' eyes.'

Horace grinned. 'Let's dazzle these devils!'

Steadying themselves with their tails, the three rats angled their plates at the cliff top. Blinding beams of sunlight bounced off the polished surfaces and into the red eyes of the attacking devils. The black beasts screeched and howled, dropping their rocks like hot potatoes as they tried to protect their eyes with their paws. Blindly, they stumbled into one another, tripping over tails and toes.

The rats were relentless. No sooner had a devil picked up a rock, than a ray of sunlight smacked him straight in the eyes. Unable to mount another attack, the furious devils retreated from the cliff top, scrambling for cover in bushes and burrows.

The three rats cheered in triumph as the last devil disappeared. Ruby lowered her plate and winked at Whisker.

'Another brilliant idea, *Fish Boy*,' she laughed. 'You're

worth your weight in silver.'

For a moment, Whisker thought she was going to give him a big hug ... or maybe even a kiss on the cheek. But then he realised they were both dangling from the top of the mast and he stank of sardines.

Hardly what every girl dreams of, he sighed.

'That was one *hell* of an escape!' Horace exclaimed. 'Devils are nearly as gruesome as vampires and ghosts – which reminds me, there's a great ghost story about a white sheet and a ...'

'I'm warning you, Horace!' Ruby broke in. 'It's a long way down.'

Horace peered over the side. 'O-on the other hand, I might s-save that story for another occasion ...'

With Devil's Cliffs behind them, the Pie Rats sailed from the shadows of the passage into a glorious sundrenched sea.

'Oh, how I love the ocean,' Horace yawned, climbing down from the mast.

'Oh, how I love the sun,' Whisker sighed.

'Don't forget silver,' Ruby mused, dropping her plates on the deck. 'Silver does have its place.'

'I'm more partial to superglue,' Pete muttered, clomping up the stairs with Fred. 'All the silver plates in the world wouldn't stop a leaky hull.'

Horace gulped. 'So, how's the hole?'

'Plugged up with *your* breakfast!' Pete sniffled. 'Three apricot pies should stop the leak – for now.'

'Can you repair the damage easily, Fred?' the Captain asked. 'We can't risk docking until we reach the island.'

'I'll need some wood,' Fred mumbled, hesitantly.

'There's an empty fireworks crate you can use,' Horace suggested.

'An extremely *big* crate, judging by last night's display,' the Captain laughed.

Fred grunted and wandered below to begin the patch up job. The rest of the crew gathered around Whisker.

'It's about time we saw those elusive items of yours, Whisker,' Pete said, tapping his pencil impatiently. 'If you haven't lost them again …'

Whisker removed the crumpled map from his left pocket and handed it to Pete. With Mr Tribble's assistance, Pete carefully unfolded the paper and laid it on the deck, awaiting the key.

Whisker took a deep breath and stuck his paw into his right pocket, half expecting to find it empty. His fingers touched the cold surface of the King's Key.

Overcome with relief, he slid the precious object from his pocket and placed it in the empty space in the centre of the map. It was a perfect fit.

'Red-berry wonder!' Horace marvelled. 'The Island of Destiny awaits us!'

'Humph!' Pete snorted, staring at the painted design. 'X marks the spot. Hardly original.'

Ruby rolled her eye. '*X, Y, Z* or a big fat letter *H*! Who cares, as long as it leads to the treasure.'

'Hey! Go easy on the *Hs*!' Horace said defensively. '*H* stands for *Horace*, you know.'

Mr Tribble pointed to the oval handle of the key. '*H* also stands for *Hope*.'

'The *Rock of Hope*,' the Captain read. 'Just as we predicted – Hope is our destination.'

'It's more than a destination,' Whisker added, running his finger over his anchor pendant. 'Hope is the key to the entire quest.'

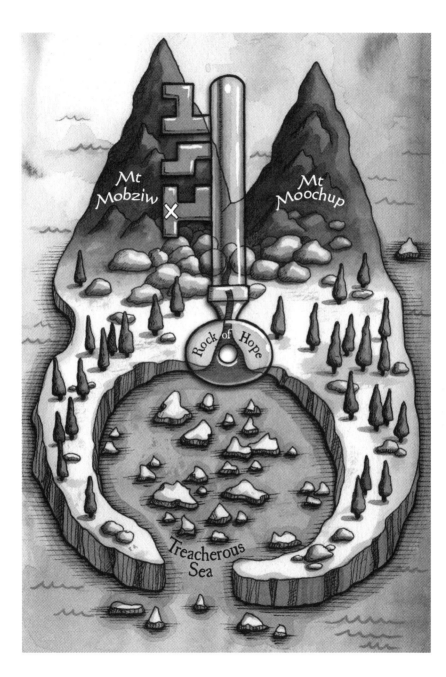

Book 3
The Island of Destiny

Armed with the King's Key and the Forgotten Map, Whisker and the Pie Rats sail to the Island of Destiny in search of the fabled treasure.

To reach the island they must first pass through the Treacherous Sea, where untold dangers lurk beneath the waves …

Discover more about the Pie Rats at:
www.pierats.com.au